I ran to the front door and saw zombies coming up the driveway. "No!" I gasped.

I sped to the back door. Zombies were climbing up the porch!

"They're everywhere!" I yelled. "There's no way out!"

Dayna rolled her eyes. "Why don't you call for help?" She handed me the phone.

"Good idea," I said. I took the receiver from her and started to dial.

Click. The line went dead.

I love Mr. Batman the dark knight.

A BOOK BY

R.L. STINE

BASED ON THE SCREENPLAY BY PATRICK READ JOHNSON

AVON BOOKS

An Imprint of Harper Collins*Publishers*

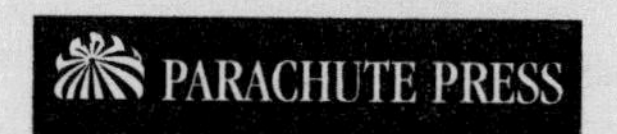

When Good Ghouls Go Bad

Printed in the United States of America.

For information address:
HarperCollins Children's Books,
a division of HarperCollins Publishers,
1350 Avenue of the Americas,
New York, NY 10019

Library of Congress Catalog Card Number: 2001117190

ISBN: 0-06-441082-X

First Avon edition, 2001

Visit us on the World Wide Web!
www.harperchildrens.com

when GOOD GHOULS go BAD

I scraped out the guts. Then I cut out his eyes, his nose, and his mouth.

There. Now it's finished, I thought. I wiped the goo off of my knife. The jack-o'-lantern I had just carved grinned up at me. It was perfect—perfectly creepy.

I picked up the pumpkin and carried it out to the porch. I set it down next to the front door, then stood back to admire the effect. It looked awesome with our other Halloween decorations. I stopped for a second to adjust the orange and black crepe-paper streamers around the doorway, then went back inside for breakfast.

Uncle Fred sat on a stool in the kitchen, reading a copy of *Sci-fi Magazine.*

"Space-food stick, Danny?" Uncle Fred offered. He waved one of his chocolate-covered energy bars under my nose. Astronauts supposedly ate them in the 1960s. Uncle Fred had kept boxes of them around ever since then.

I didn't intend to try one. I mean, they had to be stale—even if they were supposed to last forever.

"No, thanks," I said, pouring myself some cereal.

Uncle Fred sipped his Tang and stared at his half-finished plastic model on the kitchen table. When it was done, it was supposed to be a space shuttle. I wasn't sure Uncle Fred would ever finish it, though. It was taking him months.

In case you haven't figured it out by now, my uncle Fred is pretty weird. He even *looks* strange. He has bushy gray hair sticking out from his head, and the outfits he wears look more like costumes than clothes.

Today he had on his white space suit—an exact copy of the one the Apollo astronauts wore when they went to the moon in 1969. At least, that's what Uncle Fred told me. I have to take his word for it, since I'm only twelve.

The other weird thing you should know about Uncle Fred is that he isn't my uncle. He's my grandfather. But since he started the Walker Chocolate Company about a million years ago, everybody calls him Uncle Fred.

"Uncle Fred" used to be the symbol of the company, kind of like Mrs. Butterworth or that Quaker Oats guy.

The "Uncle Fred" on the chocolate box is supposed to be everybody's favorite uncle. But the *real* Uncle Fred is my closest friend. He can skateboard, play video games, and drive a go-cart as well as anybody my age. I love hanging out with him, no matter what we're doing.

I had settled down beside Uncle Fred to page through a catalog of Halloween costumes when I heard a noise out on the front porch.

"What was that?" I asked. I hurried to the door and opened it.

The sheriff's car stood in front of our house, its red and blue lights flashing. I shielded my eyes from the glare and saw Sheriff Frady loading my jack-o'-lantern into the trunk!

"Hey!" I shouted. "What are you doing?"

Sheriff Frady marched toward me. "I'm taking these decorations down, mister!" His skinny body shook, and his voice quivered as he talked. He reached over my head, and yanked the orange and black crepe paper off the front door. "You're lucky I don't arrest you!" he said, wagging the streamers in my face.

"Arrest me? Why?" I cried. "What did I do wrong?" But Sheriff Frady didn't answer me. He just stomped back to his car, shoved the streamers into the trunk, and slammed down the lid. I could see the orange and black crepe-paper ends flapping in the wind as he drove away.

I sighed and walked back inside the house.

"What's the matter, Danny?" Uncle Fred asked.

I shook my head. I didn't feel like talking to anyone about it.

Uncle Fred has lived here for *years*, I realized. And crazy stuff like this happens in Walker Falls all the time. Uncle Fred is probably used to it, I thought. But I was having a hard time adjusting.

My dad and I moved to Walker Falls, Minnesota, from Chicago a few months ago. Chicago was a big, exciting city full of interesting people. Walker Falls was a tiny, boring town full of weirdos.

After my mom and dad got divorced, Dad had this crazy idea. He wanted to fix up Walker Chocolates, the old family candy company here in town, and bring it back to life. It had been closed ever since Dad went away to college.

But for some reason, people in Walker Falls didn't seem too happy to have us back. I just wished I knew why.

The rest of the day was like every other day I'd had since we moved to Walker Falls—lousy. Mrs. Moore picked me up for school that morning. I was on her carpool route. As I boarded the minivan, the other kids shot nasty looks at me. I sat alone in the back and stared out the window.

On the way to school we passed rows and rows of boring shops and old houses. Not one house, not one shop, was decorated for Halloween, I realized. And Halloween was less than a week away!

When we arrived at school, the principal glared at me with her big bug eyes. Then the janitor tipped his bucket of soapy water over just as I was walking by. My sneakers got soaked!

I glanced back at him, and I thought I saw him smiling! As if he'd done it on purpose!

What did everybody have against me, anyway? Had I broken some kind of law by moving to this crummy town?

The worst part of the day was football practice during gym. Ryan Kankel made sure of that. And Coach Mike Kankel—Ryan's dad—didn't help.

We were about halfway into class when Tim Chadwick threw a hard pass right at me. The ball screamed toward me like a torpedo—and bounced off my chest. The hit made me lose my balance—and I tumbled to the ground. I heard the pounding of feet stampeding toward me.

Oof! Three guys threw themselves on top of me.

As I gasped for breath, Ryan and his buddy Leo hauled their beefy bodies off me.

"Fumble!" Ryan shouted so loudly, I thought my eardrums would shatter.

Coach Kankel blew his whistle. "Nice tackle,

son," he said. "Now get that loser Walker off the field."

"Sure thing, Dad," Ryan said.

I let my body go limp and pretended to pass out as Leo and some other guy carried me to the chain-link fence at the edge of the field.

Of course, I hadn't really passed out. I was just doing what I'd learned to do early on in life—play dead.

I'm not a big kid. In fact, I've always been kind of a runt. Thugs like Ryan love to pick on me. So I had to find my own way of dealing with them. The best way, I realized, is to play dead.

"Live to fight another day." That was my motto.

Of course, Dad said my motto only worked until that *other day* finally came—and you actually had to fight.

It was a good point . . . but what did Dad know? His business went bankrupt, we lost our house in Chicago, and Mom left. Now we were stuck in Walker Falls.

After a while I pretended to feel better and sat up with my back against the fence. Coach Kankel asked the school nurse to come out to the field to check me out.

I hadn't met the nurse yet. But if she was like everybody else in Walker Falls, I figured I wouldn't be getting much tender loving care.

A woman in jeans, a red shirt, and a brown jacket approached me. She smiled at me. Actually *smiled.* I realized it had been a while since a stranger had smiled at me.

"Hi, I'm Nurse Taylor Morgan," the woman said. "Are you doing okay?"

"Um—I got knocked out in football practice, Ms. Morgan," I told her.

"You can call me Taylor," she said.

She was somewhere around my dad's age, I figured, with curly brown hair and a pretty face. She took a pocket-sized flashlight from her jacket and shined it in my eyes. "I don't think you have a concussion," she said. "But we'd better call your parents. What's your name?"

"Danny Walker," I told her.

A strange look flashed across her face.

Uh-oh, I thought. *Now that she knows who I am, is she going to be mean to me?*

"Are you related to James Walker?" she asked.

"Yeah. He's my dad," I replied.

She kind of smiled, as if she were remembering something.

"Do you know him?" I asked her.

"I went to high school with him," she said. "I haven't seen him in years. Well, what's his phone number? I'll call him and see if he can come and pick you up."

I gave her Dad's work number at Walker Chocolates. He was there trying to find investors. Last I heard, he was hoping some German businessmen would come to look at the factory and help get it restarted.

Taylor pulled out a cell phone and dialed the number. I heard her say hello to Mrs. Vanderspool, my dad's assistant.

"This is Taylor Morgan, I'm the nurse at Danny's school," Taylor explained. "Could you put Mr. Walker on the phone, please?" She paused. "Yes, I'll hold."

She must have waited for about fifteen minutes. Then she hung up the phone. "Nobody picked up," she said.

Big surprise, I thought. My dad was always busy with one scheme or another. He was never around when I needed him.

Taylor bent over me. "How are you feeling now? Do you think you can go home on your own?"

I nodded. She was watching my face carefully, as if she was worried about me.

"Why don't you lie down on the grass for a bit," she suggested. "Just to make sure you're all right."

I lay back, letting the bright sunshine warm my face.

"It's hard starting over in a new town, at a new school," Taylor said. "I know how it feels. I just moved back here myself, you know."

"Really?" I asked.

She nodded. "I left town right after high school."

"Why would you want to move back to this dump?" I asked her.

She looked a little sad. "Oh, I had my reasons," she said.

I stared up at the sky for about ten minutes until the final bell rang. Then I stood up, grabbed my helmet, and started for the locker room.

"Get home safely," Taylor said. "I'll see you tomorrow."

I gave her a wave and set off to change.

When I got outside, it was such a nice day that I decided to walk home by a different route—maybe see a little more of the town. I turned the corner onto Elm Lane—and stopped short.

Elm was—well—pretty creepy.

Dead leaves fluttered down the road, collecting at my feet. A spooky old Victorian house stood in front of me, its yard overgrown with weeds and vines. Shingles and shutters dangled from the house, ready to fall at any second. The dark windows were cloaked in cobwebs.

I crossed the street to get as far away from the house as possible, and spotted a group of girls up ahead. One of them was Dayna Stenson.

Dayna was in my class. She had long brown hair and a sweet smile—not that she'd ever smiled at *me,* exactly. Whenever I saw her, I couldn't stop looking at her.

Dayna waved goodbye to her friends and started in the direction of the old Victorian house I'd just passed. As she walked by me, I glanced away. Then I turned around to look at her some more—and walked right into a lamppost.

Bam! I collapsed to the ground for the second time that day.

I climbed unsteadily to my feet, picked up my book bag, and glanced back to check if Dayna had seen me fall. No. She was gone.

It was beginning to get dark. I started to pick up my pace. Then I saw what was coming up ahead.

The cemetery.

I gulped. There was no way to avoid it. I'd have to walk past it to get home.

Relax, man, I coached myself. Ghosts don't really float around in cemeteries. That stuff's only in the movies.

I straightened up and marched briskly toward the graveyard.

Dusk was falling as I reached the old iron fence. It was too dark to see well—but still too light for the streetlights to come on. I tried not to look inside at the rows of old graves lined up beyond that fence. They made me think about zombies, ghouls, and all kinds of undead creatures.

I walked faster.

Up ahead I could see the entrance to the cemetery. That meant I was halfway past. Keep moving, I coached myself. Almost there.

Out of the corner of my eye I noticed that the cemetery gate was ajar.

I swallowed hard and continued walking.

That's when a huge, dark figure leaped out at me. "Boo!" it shouted.

I let out a high-pitched shriek.

Wait a minute. A real ghost wouldn't say "Boo," I realized.

I was right. The dark figure in front of me wasn't a ghost. It was much scarier than that.

It was Ryan Kankel.

Ryan Kankel.

What rotten luck.

Behind him stood his henchman, Leo. I tried to act cool.

"Boo?" I said, squinting at them. "Is that the best you could come up with?"

Ryan scowled at Leo. "Yeah, you jerk."

"So, what's up?" I asked, trying to sound calm.

"Your number, that's what's up," Ryan growled.

Leo and Ryan each grabbed one of my arms and marched me into the cemetery. My heart started to thump hard in my chest.

"Ryan, why can't you just leave me alone?" I asked. "I already gave you my snack-pack pudding for lunch and my glow-in-the-dark pen. Plus I let you play target practice with me during gym, remember? What more do you want? What did I do to you? Why are you so mad at me?"

"I'm not mad at you, Danny," Ryan said. He flashed me a nasty grin. "I'm *concerned* about you."

"Concerned?" I echoed.

Ryan nodded. "You see, Walker, you're different. And in a big city like Chicago, that might be a good thing. But here in Walker Falls, being different can get you hurt—or worse."

They dragged me through the graveyard. We passed line after line of crumbling, creepy tombstones. Then we stopped in front of a small, old concrete building. Ryan and Leo let go of my arms.

The building was shaped like a tiny rectangle with a rusted iron door. A thick chain was threaded through the handles of the door. It was held in place by a heavy metal lock. Vines sprouted out of the cracks and crevices in the concrete walls.

Why did they bring me here? I wondered.

"Know what this is, Danny?" Ryan asked.

"A sepulcher?" I said.

Leo snickered as if I'd just said a nasty word.

"Wrong," Ryan snorted. "Try again, brainiac."

"A crypt?" I ventured.

"No, jerk!" Ryan cried. "It's a place where they bury somebody!"

"Oh, really?" I said, trying hard not to roll my eyes. I couldn't stand people who were so stupid they didn't even know they were stupid. But I seemed to run into a lot of them in this town.

"And this particular place where they bury somebody happens to have a very special somebody buried in it. Or should I say—what's *left* of somebody." Ryan paused dramatically. "His name is CURTIS DANKO!"

Leo gulped nervously.

"Ever hear of him, Danny?" Ryan asked.

"No," I replied.

"Well, then, I'll tell you all about him," Ryan offered. "Curtis Danko was an eighth grader at Walker Falls Middle School way back in 1981. That's twenty years ago. Just like you, Danny, he was different. . . ."

As Ryan told the story, I tried to picture it all in my mind. I saw Curtis Danko slinking through the halls of Walker Falls Middle School.

He was pale and thin and had big dark eyes with dark rings around them. His black hair was frizzy and wild. All the other kids avoided him. They wouldn't even look him in the eye.

But he didn't pay any attention to them. He was busy with his own thoughts, lost in his own world.

"He couldn't play sports," Ryan told me. "He couldn't fight. He didn't have a girlfriend. And he never wanted to do what all the other kids wanted to do. In art class, when all the other kids would paint pictures of normal stuff like barns and tractors and baskets of apples, Curtis Danko would paint pictures of monsters or aliens."

I could see Curtis in art class, sitting separately from the other kids. Twenty years ago Coach Kankel, Ryan's father, was probably in the eighth grade. With Marge Vanderspool, my father's assistant. And Sheriff Frady. I bet they all knew Curtis Danko.

My dad was a few years older, though. He would have already gone away to college by then.

Coach Kankel was probably just like Ryan in those days, I thought. A big bully. Come to think of it, he's just like Ryan *now*.

"One day," Ryan continued, "the city council announced that they wanted to put up a statue in the town square for the big Halloween celebration. They asked all the eighth graders to make sculptures of their heroes, and the town would vote on which one they liked best. The sculpture that got the most votes would be made into a real statue and placed on the pedestal in the town square."

"Yeah, yeah, Ryan. This story is getting scarier by the minute," I said. "What does this have to do with me being here in the graveyard with you?"

"I'm getting to that," Ryan snapped. "All the normal kids worked on their sculptures during the school day. They kept them out in the open, where everyone could see them. My dad did a great sculpture of *his* dad," Ryan bragged. "But Curtis Danko kept his sculpture covered up. He wouldn't show it to anyone."

I imagined Curtis Danko, sitting alone on the far side of the room, staring straight ahead with his dark, blank eyes. His sculpture stood next to him, covered with a canvas cloth secured with bike chains and padlocks.

"Curtis refused to work on his sculpture during art class because he didn't want anyone to see it," Ryan continued. "So he sneaked into the art room at night, all alone. He knew he'd be caught if he turned on the light. So he brought jars of fireflies with him to light his way. No one ever saw his sculpture—not until Halloween night, 1981.

"That's when my dad and some of his friends sneaked up to the school at night, dressed in their Halloween costumes," Ryan went on. "Dad glanced up at the art room window and saw a green glow coming from it. The fireflies. He knew Curtis was up there, working on his statue.

"Dad placed a ladder against the school wall. It knocked against the art room window.

"In the art room Curtis must have heard a noise. Something bumping against the window. He probably grabbed his statue, looking around the room for a place to hide. But the only decent hiding place was the kiln room.

"The kiln room was like a big oven. The art teacher put the students' sculptures in there to bake when they were done.

"Curtis must have slipped into the kiln room and shut the door just as the door to the art room opened and the janitor came in to clean the room. That's when my dad and his buddies climbed the ladder, saw the janitor, and left.

"No one knows how the kiln door got locked," Ryan said. "Or why Curtis never shouted for anyone to let him out . . . or how the kiln got turned on all by itself . . . or why no one ever heard his screams . . .

"But the next day, when my dad got to the art room, he noticed that something was wrong. It was very hot in there. So my dad went to the kiln. His eyes grew wide when he saw that the door was barred. The gas gauge on the furnace read Empty. And the furnace button was on!"

Next to Ryan, Leo's teeth were chattering. I stood perfectly still, waiting to hear the end of the story.

"When my dad opened the kiln door," Ryan said, "and looked inside . . . all that was left of Curtis Danko was his burned-up skeleton . . . his finished sculpture . . . and a message, written in the ashes at his bony feet."

I gasped, realizing I had stopped breathing for a few seconds. "What did the message say?" I whispered.

Ryan leaned closer. "It said, 'If you ever have

another Halloween, I will return and destroy you all!'"

Leo covered his eyes with his hands.

"And since that day, twenty years ago, Walker Falls has never had another Halloween," Ryan finished.

I snapped back to the present. Ryan's piggish face had a smug smile on it. The story explained a lot. Like why people treated me like a criminal for putting a jack-o'-lantern on my front porch.

"That's crazy," I said. "You don't really believe Curtis Danko can come back and destroy you—do you?"

"Oh, yes, we do," Ryan insisted. "And you want to know why? Because Curtis Danko's statue was so horrible that my father was blind for three days after he looked at it. He said that only someone truly evil could have made it. My dad covered that statue up so no one else would feel the searing pain that just one glimpse of it brought to his eyes."

"Oh, please." I sighed. How could a whole town believe such a stupid story?

"It's true!" Ryan insisted. "When my dad told people what the statue looked like under that shroud, nobody dared to see it for themselves. They just carted it off, covered in its shroud. Then they buried it—with Curtis—*in there.*" He pointed at the crypt.

I glanced up at Curtis Danko's dark crypt, looming before me. Ryan grabbed me by the sweatshirt and pulled my face so close to his I could smell the sloppy joes on his breath.

"And now," he said, "you're going to go in there—to look at the statue yourself."

Ryan gave me a push toward the crypt. "Go look at the statue!" he ordered.

I gulped. Maybe the Curtis Danko story was silly—but I still didn't want to go inside somebody's grave!

"Um . . . why am I doing this, exactly?" I asked, turning back to face him.

"Because I want to know what it really looks like!" Ryan said.

"So why don't you go look at it yourself?" I asked.

"I would—but what if one peek at it makes me burst into flames? Or turn to stone? Or makes my head explode? I want someone to try it out ahead of me."

"I see." I nodded, stalling for time. "So why don't you send in the jerk?" I gestured toward Leo.

Ryan rolled his eyes. "What kind of description

could I get from him? He's an idiot! *You* will tell me exactly what it looks like. *If* you survive. . ."

Ka-chink! I heard a noise that sounded like a heavy chain hitting dirt. I spun around to see the chain on the ground and the lock in Leo's hand. In the other hand he waved the key. Ryan gave me a mean grin.

I glanced at the rusty crypt door. They don't really expect me to go in there, I thought. Do they?

The two bullies took a step toward me. Then another step.

Yes, I realized. They did.

I looked at the crypt again. Then I turned and bolted.

"Get him!" Ryan shouted.

I raced through the maze of gravestones and crypts. I stopped just once to glance back. Leo was after me!

And for such a bulky guy, he was a pretty fast runner. I hurried through the dark graveyard, trying to find the gate. I looked left and right. Where was it? Why couldn't I find it?

Leo began to catch up. I could hear his panting breaths behind me. Up ahead I saw the bars of the cemetery fence. I raced straight for them. The bars were set pretty narrow, but I'm small so I thought I could squeeze through them.

I reached the fence just as Leo's hand grazed my

shoulder. I twisted sideways and slipped between the bars. I looked back to see Leo slam into the fence. Yes! He'd never fit through the bars. He turned and hurried toward the gate.

I ran all the way home, leaped up the porch steps, grabbed the doorknob, and turned it.

Oh, no! It was locked!

Behind me I heard sneakers beating the sidewalk. The doofus was catching up!

I banged on the door once, twice—then turned to see Leo running up the porch steps.

This is it, I thought. He's going to pound me into hamburger! I pressed my back against the door—and it opened!

I tumbled backward into the foyer. Landed on my back. A tall man wearing armor and a horned silver helmet leaned over me.

He raised a razor-sharp ax over his head and screamed out a terrifying battle cry! "AAAAIIIEEEEE-YYYAAAHHH!"

The ax glinted in the porch light. I shut my eyes and screamed as it came down to chop off my head.

The ax swished past my face, missing me by inches. I opened my eyes.

Leo had stopped in his tracks. He took one look at the armored warrior, shrieked, and ran for his life.

I looked up at the warrior towering over me and screamed again. The warrior laughed.

That's when I noticed the bushy gray hair sticking out from under the helmet.

"Uncle Fred?" I asked.

"That's Galwrath the Executioner to you, my wee lad!" Uncle Fred answered in a thick Scottish brogue.

I smiled as he reached down, grabbed my hand, and pulled me to my feet. He led me inside the house, hollering and whooping and slashing at make-believe enemies with his ax.

Thwong! With one powerful swing Uncle Fred buried the ax blade in the wall.

"Whoops!" he said, his face blushing. He struggled to yank the ax out, tearing up bits of wallpaper and plaster in the process. But it wouldn't budge.

"Oh, well," he said, giving up. "I never liked that wallpaper anyway." He left the ax sticking out of the wall.

I followed him into the living room, winding my way through my unpacked boxes of toys and sports equipment. Uncle Fred took off his warrior helmet and tossed it to the floor.

He settled down at the kitchen table and started to work on his space shuttle model. I grabbed a banana and sat on the kitchen counter to eat it.

"So who was that little mutant chasing you, Danny?" he asked.

I didn't want to worry Uncle Fred. "Some kid from school. We were just fooling. Where's Dad?" I asked, changing the subject. "He promised we'd start making our Halloween costumes tonight."

Uncle Fred frowned. "He said something about working late on his big 'Halloween Spooktacular.'" Uncle Fred waved his hands in the air when he said "Spooktacular." I could tell by his tone of voice he thought that whatever it was, it was a silly reason to skip making Halloween costumes.

I slumped. Dad was always working late—or something. If he promised to come home and help me make a costume, I could pretty much bet it wouldn't happen. Anyway, Dad already had a costume, I thought to myself. He was the Invisible Man.

Later that night Uncle Fred tried to cheer me up by setting up his old Hot Wheels track. He had some cool new cars and some of the original ones from the sixties.

"Which car do you want?" Uncle Fred asked me, offering me his two best racers. "The Red Baron or the Dodge Viper?"

I studied the track Uncle Fred had set up in the foyer. It was a tangle of orange plastic loops and curves, starting with a steep downhill plunge and ending with a jump—right through the mail slot in the front door.

"I'll take the Viper," I decided.

"Good choice," Uncle Fred said, handing me the little toy car. "It's more aerodynamic. But the Baron is a classic."

We crouched by the beginning of the track, ready to race, when the front door burst open. It was Dad.

"The Germans are coming! The Germans are coming!" he shouted happily.

"No need to panic!" Uncle Fred said, standing up. "Danny, you get my old army helmet from the attic! I'll go out and see if I can borrow a tank somewhere!"

I thought I saw Dad's eyes flash with anger at Uncle Fred's joke. But it happened so quickly, I couldn't be sure.

"You know that's not what I meant," Dad said. "The German investors have agreed to come to Walker Falls and look at Walker Chocolates. If they'll invest in the factory, I think we can make it work again."

"Whoopee," Uncle Fred said, not smiling.

"You know, I worked hard to make this happen," my dad said. "Real hard."

Uncle Fred rolled his eyes. "Don't we know it."

Dad set down his briefcase and pointed at Uncle Fred. "I'm just following your example. You always said, 'You've got to make your mark in this world.' Remember—*'Uncle Fred'*?" He scowled and went into the kitchen.

"There's more than one way to leave a mark, Jamie!" Uncle Fred called after him. "Being a big success is no guarantee of being a good father."

"At least we agree on that," Dad called back. He picked up some videotapes from the kitchen counter and headed into the living room. I ran after him.

"Dad!" I cried. "Wait!"

Dad was planning a "Halloween Spooktacular" in a town where people thought that if they celebrated Halloween they'd all *die.* Chances were, the

Spooktacular wasn't the best idea for getting the town behind the factory. I had to tell him about Curtis Danko!

"Running late, Danny," Dad said. "I've got to make a presentation at the town meeting tonight." He picked up the presentation he had made—a scale model of the Walker Falls town square. "I just stopped by for a second to pick up some things. Whatever it is, it'll have to wait."

He started back toward the foyer. I followed him. If I didn't stop him, this presentation was going to be a big mistake.

"But there's this kid—" I began, trying to think of a way to tell him the whole story. "You should hear what he said about Hallo—"

"If someone's bothering you at school," Dad interrupted, "just—"

"No!" I cut in. "This kid is *dead*!"

"Violence never solves anything, Danny," Dad said. He opened the front door and stepped out onto the porch.

"But, Dad—" I called, wishing he'd stop and listen to me. He hurried down the front steps.

At the bottom he turned around to face me. "Trust me, son," he said, walking backward toward his car. "Things are going to get better. After tonight the name Walker is going to mean something in this town again."

He got into his car and sped away.

Uncle Fred put a hand on my shoulder. "Hey," he said. "You want to see what your dad is up to? I've got an idea." He led me into the house.

"But first we have to make Halloween come a little early this year," he whispered in my ear.

Uncle Fred and I arrived at the town hall just before the meeting got started. No one recognized us—not even Dad. And for good reason. Uncle Fred was dressed up like an old lady in a wig and a skirt. And he'd made *me* dress up like a girl!

He'd slapped a Dorothy from *The Wizard of Oz* wig—with two long brown braids—on my head. He'd even put a little lipstick on me.

"If anyone recognizes me, I'm running away from home," I warned him. *"Forever."*

"Don't worry, no one will," Uncle Fred assured me. "I do this all the time."

The parking lot was packed with cars. I noticed brand-new bumper stickers on back of each one—some that said RE-ELECT MAYOR CHURNEY and others that said KANKEL FOR MAYOR.

Yeah, Coach Kankel was running for mayor. To me, that was scarier than the story about Curtis Danko.

It seemed as if the whole town had shown up for the meeting. People perched on clattering folding chairs, glaring up toward the stage. Mayor Churney, owner of Churney's—the biggest store in town—took his place at the podium.

Uncle Fred led me all the way to the front row, where we sat down. At one side of the stage I noticed Dad talking to the school nurse, Taylor Morgan. On the other I noticed Coach Kankel, frowning.

Mayor Churney wiped his sweaty forehead with a handkerchief. "All right, folks. I know what you're thinking—a town meeting means bad news, right? Well, guess what? We have a special guest tonight who has come up with what he tells me is a surefire solution to our town's money problems."

"He's lowering the prices at Churney's department store?" someone yelled from the back.

Mayor Churney pretended to laugh. "Heh heh heh . . . funny . . . Anyway, here he is—James Walker."

Mayor Churney left the stage. Dad approached the microphone. No one clapped.

Dad cleared his throat. "Thank you, Mr. Mayor. And hello again, Walker Falls!"

No one said a word.

I glanced back at the audience. They all stared at Dad suspiciously.

"I, uh . . ." Dad fumbled with his notes. I could see he was nervous. I felt a little sorry for him.

"I say 'hello again' because, though most of you don't know me, I actually grew up in this town," he continued.

The crowd was still silent, waiting. Uncle Fred unwrapped a space-food stick and took a bite.

"Some of you may remember me as little Jamie Walker," Dad went on. "I used to t.p. some of your houses on Hallowee—"

Suddenly the crowd erupted into a chorus of throat-clearing and coughs. Dad paused. "Hallo—"

The crowd sputtered and coughed again, loudly. Dad looked offstage at Mayor Churney. The mayor shrugged as if he didn't know what was going on. I had the feeling that wasn't true.

Dad gave up and went on with his talk. "Yes, well. As some of you may also remember, Walker Chocolates was once the fifth most successful producer of chocolate in America!"

I was surprised. I'd never realized Walker Chocolates had been such a big company. Dad beamed as if he expected applause, but it didn't come.

"Tell us something we don't know!" someone heckled from the back of the room.

"Yeah!" another voice called out. "Like why your old man just went and shut the factory down on us!"

I glanced at Uncle Fred, but he wouldn't look at

me. He stopped chewing on his space-food stick for a second and stared at the purse in his lap. I noticed some of the older people squirming uncomfortably in their seats.

Dad said, "I don't know why my father shut the factory down. He never told anyone—not even me. But whatever the reason, I'm sure it was the most painful decision of his life. Because I know he loved that chocolate company." Dad paused. The room was silent.

"My father didn't go into the candy business because he thought he'd get rich," Dad continued. "He did it because it made people happy. And the one time of the year it made them happiest was Halloween."

The crowd gasped. A man in the back shouted, "Holy smokes! He said it! He said Hallo—"

"Well, for crying out loud, Hank, don't say it *again*!" Sheriff Frady barked.

Dad blinked and looked confused. I couldn't believe what I was hearing. It was one thing when a dopey kid like Ryan Kankel believed in a Halloween curse. But the whole town? Was everyone *really* afraid just to say the word *Halloween*?

The crowd quieted down to let Dad finish what he had to say. "When I moved back to town," he said, "I started thinking about all the happy memories from my childhood, when the factory was working night and day. . . . People would head down to Jonathan's pumpkin patch and carve jack-o'-lanterns and kids would start making their costumes. . . . Our entire lives were dedicated to one night of pranks and first kisses and the biggest reward of all—a big fat bag of candy!"

I spotted Taylor Morgan standing near the stage. She had a dreamy look on her face, as if she were remembering the same happy Halloweens as Dad.

"The more I thought about those days," Dad said, "the more I wanted to have them back. And that's why I decided to start the factory up again."

The crowd murmured in surprise. Coach Kankel glared angrily at Dad. Why would he care if Dad reopened the chocolate factory? I wondered. Did he have something against candy? Or was he just mean?

"Folks, the machines are oiled and ready," Dad announced. "The ingredients are in the hoppers. My assistant, Mrs. Vanderspool, and I ran a test batch of the old recipe to see if it was as good as we remembered."

Mrs. Vanderspool, a friendly-looking woman, stood up with a basket of candy bars and began to hand them out. She had a nervous smile plastered on her face, as if she were afraid the mob would turn against her just for giving out candy. A lot of people in the crowd refused to touch the candy bars, but a few people nodded and took one. Mrs. Vanderspool stopped in front of Uncle Fred and me with her basket. After giving us a funny look, she said, "Would you like to try a Walker Chocolate bar, miss?"

"Thank you," I said, trying to make my voice high like a girl's. I took a piece of chocolate and tasted it. It was delicious! I couldn't believe my own dad knew how to make candy this good.

"All I need to get started," Dad said over the murmuring of the crowd, "are people to make the factory work."

Coach Kankel stood up and shouted, "You folks really want to get involved with the Walkers again? Don't forget—this is the son of that greedy old man who cut and run and left us high and dry."

I glanced at Uncle Fred, and again he stared at his lap. The crowd grumbled in agreement with Coach Kankel.

Dad pounded on the podium for attention. "My father was anything but greedy," he insisted. "He paid every one of the people who worked for him a good wage. He gave whatever he could to help people in need. He even built the band shell in the town square so he could take my mother and all their friends dancing with the fireflies on summer nights. I remember seeing more than one of you out there with them. . . ."

Uncle Fred stirred in his seat. I spotted a tiny

tear sparkling in the corner of his eye. I barely remembered my grandmother, but I could see that Uncle Fred must have loved her.

"Look," Dad said, "I can't explain my father's actions. But if you help me—maybe I can make up for what he did."

A squeaky voice shouted out, "What's the catch?" I glanced around, trying to figure out who had called out, when I realized it was Uncle Fred. One of the many things he's good at is throwing his voice.

Dad didn't seem to have any idea who had shouted to him. "The catch," he said to the crowd, "is that I've spent everything I've got just to get to this point. And in order to pay the workers at Walker Chocolates, I need to bring in some investors. I need to find someone who can see what I see when I look at that old factory up there. So I've invited some very wealthy German investors to come to Walker Falls on October thirty-first—"

The crowd stirred. A woman in the back gasped, "Oh, no!" She grabbed her three children by the hand and hustled out of the hall.

Sheriff Frady asked, "Excuse me, Mr. Walker, but is there any particular reason you chose that particular day?"

"Well—" Dad began.

"Gee—I wonder if it's because that's the night

the 'Kankel for Mayor' committee is holding its Silent Auction fund-raiser and Octoberfest!" Coach Kankel barked.

"No—actually, I chose that date because it's Halloween!" Dad replied.

"AAAAH! He said it again!" people cried.

"Because it's time to trick or treat!" Dad said.

"Stop him!" someone shrieked. "Somebody *do* something!"

"I've got a warehouse full of costumes and masks and pumpkins and candles and glow-in-the-dark paper skeletons sitting up there at the factory," Dad said.

The crowd was going crazy with fear. But Dad didn't understand. He seemed to think they *liked* the idea of Halloween, and he wouldn't stop talking about it!

"With your help," he shouted over gasps of horror, "I'll be bringing those Germans to town for our first annual—" He took a deep breath, then held a remote control clicker in one hand and shouted, "HALLOWEEN NIGHT SPOOKTACULAR!"

He clicked the remote control and turned to face a big screen behind him. Spooky organ music and haunted house sound effects filled the hall. On the screen, Dad showed slides of ghouls, ghosts, and goblins.

Dad didn't even notice as everybody in the hall

leaped to their feet screaming, running out of the building as fast as they could. By the time he turned around again, the only people left were me, Uncle Fred, and Taylor Morgan.

"Uncle Fred," I asked. "What is everybody so afraid of? And why do they hate us?"

"You'll learn why," Uncle Fred said. "Our family has a dark, dark secret. And you'll learn it . . . soon enough."

Uncle Fred didn't tell me the family secret right then and there—but I had a feeling it had something to do with the curse of Curtis Danko.

"Why didn't you tell me?" Dad cried. He sat sprawled in a chair in the living room, surrounded by his sketches and props for the Spooktacular. He was pressing his fists against his eyes and he looked miserable. "Why didn't you tell me about Curtis Danko?"

Uncle Fred and I sat on the couch. We had both taken off our wigs, but we still wore our dresses. I couldn't wait to change out of mine, but Dad was so mad at Uncle Fred, I was afraid to leave them alone together.

"Well, you were in college—out of town when it happened. And we all know how much you hate bad news," Uncle Fred joked. I could tell he felt bad, but he was trying to cheer Dad up.

"Curtis Danko isn't bad news!" Dad cried. "Curtis Danko is the END OF THE WORLD!"

"That's pretty much what Curtis Danko said, too," Uncle Fred murmured.

"Oh, come on!" Dad snapped. "You don't really believe he's going to rise from his grave and kill everybody in town, do you?"

I looked at Uncle Fred to see what he'd say. I wasn't sure what he believed—but I had a feeling maybe he *did* believe in ghosts.

He sat very quietly for a few seconds, staring at an old photograph on the mantel—a picture taken on the day he married my grandmother.

"I believe that the spirits of the dearly departed linger for a while," he said softly. "To make sure the people they love get on with their lives. . . . But the not-so-dearly departed stay longer—to take care of unfinished business of a darker kind."

I shivered as I sat beside him, following his gaze out the window toward the cemetery in the distance.

"I'll tell you what I believe," Dad said, sitting up in his chair. "I believe I saw hope in the eyes of a lot of people in that crowd—and excitement in the eyes of their kids. I believe if this town woke up and found all our Halloween Spooktacular stuff put up, they'd get caught up in it—in spite of their fears."

"You're a dreamer, Jamie," Uncle Fred said. Dad glanced at me, and I shrugged. I thought I'd seen a lot more fear in the townspeople than excitement. But I didn't want to let Dad down. I could tell his plan meant so much to him.

"You were a dreamer, too, once upon a time," Dad said to Uncle Fred. "I don't understand what happened to you. The Uncle Fred I used to know was responsible—a leader. He built his house with his bare hands. He built that factory over there. . . . He built a town and a fortune and—"

"He also built that kiln room," Uncle Fred said.

Dad and I both stared at him. I couldn't believe it! My own grandfather had built the kiln room—where Curtis Danko died!

Was *that* our family's dark secret? I thought. Was that why no one in town liked us? Because they thought we were responsible for the curse of Curtis Danko?

"There's a fine line between dreams and nightmares," Uncle Fred finished. "You'd better be careful, Jamie. I know you mean well. But sometimes your dreams can get out of hand—and cause terrible trouble for everyone."

Dad scowled. He stood up and stalked out of the room, kicking the scale model of the town square out of his way as he left.

• • •

I couldn't fall asleep that night. I lay on my bed in Dad's old room and stared at all his childhood toys. His old posters still hung on the walls, and his shelves were filled with models he had made when he was a boy. The best one was a big scale model of the Apollo Saturn moon rocket perched on a desk in the corner of the room. The Apollo space rocket had gone to the moon in 1969. I knew my Dad must have thought that was cool. I could tell he'd worked hard on the model—it was a complicated one.

I'd left my window open a crack, and late in the night, after I had finally fallen asleep, a breeze blew through it, rustling my hair. I turned over and saw two tiny greenish-yellow lights flickering in the room. What were they?

Fireflies, I realized as they hovered over my face.

Wait—fireflies? In October? How could that be?

The cold breeze grew stronger. Dead leaves blew through the window, rustling across my comforter.

I sat up, trying to pull the comforter tighter around me—and screamed!

I wasn't in my room. I was in the cemetery!

The moonlight glowed on the rows of gravestones surrounding me. Jack-o'-lanterns floated through the air, ghosts hovered in the trees, and the bones of skeletons glowed in the moonlight.

My heart raced in horror. I spun around and saw a huge stone pedestal towering over me. On top of it stood a giant statue, covered in a rotten canvas shroud and wrapped in a tangle of twine. The two fireflies flitted around the statue, landing near the top—where a head might be.

The wind whipped like a tornado, whirling faster and faster. I tried to back away from the statue. I didn't want to see it whatever was under that shroud. But the figure under the shroud began to move! It wriggled and twisted under the sheet, as if it were alive.

I tried to turn and run but the wind held me in place. A bolt of lightning flashed over the statue as it writhed, struggling to break out of the twine that bound it.

Snap! Snap! Snap! The bits of twine began to break away. The statue was freeing itself! The canvas shroud billowed out and started to lift off. The wind pushed me closer and closer to the statue. Then it blew the shroud off!

"Nooooo!" I screamed as I tried to close my eyes. But it was too late.

I stared at the statue—but all I saw was the color white. I glanced from side to side and realized I was staring up at my bedroom ceiling. My white bedroom ceiling.

Sweating, I sat up in bed. Morning! It was morning. The cemetery was gone! The whole thing had been a horrible dream!

Still shaking with fear, I hauled myself out of bed and padded downstairs to the kitchen, in my pajamas. Uncle Fred stood at the table, dressed in his space suit. He was stuffing things into a big backpack—underwear, socks, a blender, a box of Pop-Tarts.

"Uncle Fred—what are you doing?" I asked.

Uncle Fred jammed a handful of space-food sticks into the backpack and tried to close the top flap. Then he sat down at the table and sighed.

"You know," he began, "when your dad was

your age, he always wanted to go to Cape Kennedy to see an Apollo moon rocket blast off. He even loaded the trunk of the old car with space-food sticks and Tang for the trip. And I always said, 'Hey, that's a great idea, sport—as soon as I'm finished going over these inventory reports, we'll start planning that trip.' But I never got around to finishing those inventory reports."

He stood up and threw the backpack over his shoulder. He looked me straight in the eye. *Oh, no,* I thought. *He's leaving!*

"I read in the paper today that the space shuttle is blasting off next week," Uncle Fred said. "I figure the space-food sticks and Tang your dad put in the car back in the sixties are still good. And if I drive day and night, I'll get there in time to get a good seat down on the beach. Want to come along?"

Was he really going down to Florida to see a shuttle blast off? It sounded crazy—and I wanted to go more than anything. But I knew I couldn't. "I've got school," I reminded him.

"I'll write you a note," he offered.

"They won't take it," I said. "You're not my dad."

"Yeah." Uncle Fred sighed. "I guess that's true." But in a way, I wished he *were* my dad. And I know he wished I were his son. I think he wanted a second chance to be a good father.

Uncle Fred started for the front door. "Hey, I'll

be back—sooner or later," he said, reaching for the doorknob. "Just take care of my Hot Wheels for me. Okay?"

I swallowed hard and nodded. He opened the door and we stepped out onto the front porch. I blinked for a few seconds in the bright sunlight. Uncle Fred froze beside me.

I gasped when I realized our front yard was full of people—people carrying torches and rakes. It looked as if the whole town had shown up—and they were angry.

"What have we done now?" I asked.

"Uh—we do our own landscaping," Uncle Fred joked.

The crowd waved their rakes and glared at us. Coach Kankel stepped to the front of the crowd. "What's the matter with you people?" he demanded. "We told you we didn't want anything to do with your Hallow—"

"SHHHHH!" the crowd hissed.

"Your Hallo-you-know-what!" Coach Kankel said. "And what do you do? You go ahead and set it up anyway—in the middle of the night!"

I blinked and gazed up at Uncle Fred. What was Coach Kankel talking about?

Uncle Fred and I stepped off the porch and glanced down the street. "Wow!" I gasped. The entire block was covered with Halloween decorations! Every house had at least one jack-o'-lantern on its front porch, and the front doors were plastered with paper skeletons, witches, ghosts, and orange and black crepe paper.

I looked over at Uncle Fred again, and he shrugged. But this time there was a twinkle in his eye that made me wonder—who had done this? Was it Dad? Or Uncle Fred?

Some of our neighbors were frantically tearing the decorations down. Others just stared at their Halloween houses in disbelief. But all the kids looked excited and happy—as if it were Christmas morning. *They've never had Halloween,* I realized, feeling sorry for them. It wasn't their fault they were born in the most nervous town ever.

Sheriff Frady pulled up in his patrol car, siren wailing. He stuck his head out the open front window and shouted, "Hey, everybody! Wait till you see what they put up in front of the town hall!"

I dashed inside the house to throw on some clothes. Then Uncle Fred and I followed the mob downtown to the town square.

There, right in the middle, stood the biggest pile of pumpkins I'd ever seen. A huge mountain that reached all the way to the roof of the town hall. It was like a small Egyptian pyramid.

Uncle Fred and I pushed through the crowd to the front. I found myself standing right next to

Dayna Stenson. I glanced at her quickly—and thought I saw her looking at me and smiling.

A little girl who stood between her parents stared at the mountain of pumpkins. She pointed at it and cried out, "What is it?"

"It's a miracle," Mayor Churney murmured.

"It's a warning," Coach Kankel barked.

Uncle Fred rolled his eyes. "It's a pile of pumpkins!" he shouted, as if he'd never seen such stupid people in his whole life. "A big, beautiful, *impossible* pile of pumpkins!"

The little girl tugged on her mother's sleeve. "Mommy! Can we get a pumpkin?"

Her mother shook her head. "No, honey. Remember Curtis Danko—"

"Aw, what the heck," the little girl's father said. "I mean, Curtis Danko didn't say, 'If you ever buy another pumpkin—'" He stamped his foot defiantly and added, "We haven't had pumpkin pie in twenty years!"

"What's pumpkin pie?" the little girl asked.

I gazed at the huge pile of pumpkins while the townspeople fussed over it. It was one of the coolest things I'd ever seen. The sun glowed warm on the orange pumpkin skins, and for the first time since I'd moved to Walker Falls the town square felt like a good place to be.

I felt an arm rest on my shoulder—Uncle Fred.

He smiled down at me, that twinkle in his eyes again. I smiled back. Now I was sure Uncle Fred was behind this, and I knew he'd done it—for Dad. For Dad and for the whole town.

Uncle Fred started toward the pumpkin pile. It was so tall it cast a long shadow over the square. He stood in the shadow and stared at the murmuring crowd. Then I saw him smile at someone.

I followed his gaze and spotted Dad standing at the edge of the crowd. Dad smiled back at him.

Uncle Fred turned to the pile of pumpkins. He bent down and picked out a big, fat pumpkin from the bottom of the pile. He heaved it over his head and shouted, "Happy Halloween!"

I cheered. Then I heard it. Something rumbling behind Uncle Fred. At first I thought it was thunder, but there wasn't a cloud in the sky that day.

A small pumpkin rolled down the pile and bounced at Uncle Fred's feet.

Uncle Fred's face grew pale as he turned to stare at the pyramid. Pumpkins began to roll down, faster and faster. The rumble grew louder and louder until it was an earsplitting roar!

My heart leaped to my throat. The pile was falling apart! It was a pumpkin avalanche! And Uncle Fred stood right in its path!

An orange tidal wave crashed down on Uncle Fred. Pumpkins flooded the town square, rolling along the ground like bowling balls. The crowd scattered—all except for me, Dad, and Dayna. I stood frozen in place, screaming until my throat was raw.

Uncle Fred disappeared beneath the pile of pumpkins. He was completely buried!

One last, enormous pumpkin rolled toward me and stopped at my feet. I stared at it. Dad and Dayna stared at it, too.

The pumpkin had been deformed, pressed into a new shape. It looked like a mask, inside out, in the shape of a terrified, screaming face—Uncle Fred's face.

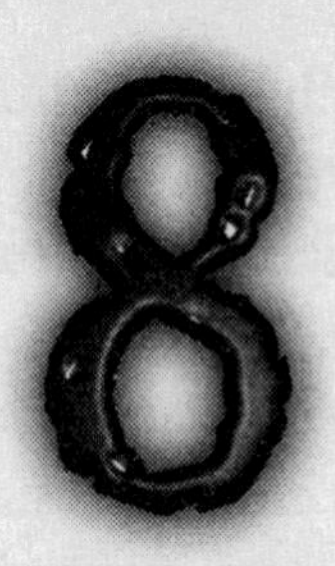

"Frederick Walker's life was not in vain," the minister droned. I shifted uncomfortably from one foot to the other as he continued with the sermon.

I was standing in the cemetery on the day before Halloween, wearing my navy blue suit and Uncle Fred's Apollo space helmet. I kept the visor down.

Uncle Fred's funeral drew a large crowd. Mayor Churney and Mrs. Vanderspool, Dad's secretary, stood on either side of Dad. Nearby I spotted Coach Kankel, Sheriff Frady, Taylor Morgan, Dayna Stenson, and a bunch of kids from school with their parents. I was amazed that so many people came to see Uncle Fred when he was dead. Most of them wouldn't give him the time of day while he was alive.

The big hole I was staring down at was Uncle Fred's grave. I couldn't believe my grandfather lay in that coffin. I didn't know what I was going to do without him.

"He was a gentle man, beloved by all whose lives he touched," the minister said. Coach Kankel cleared his throat.

"Well, until certain events," the reverend corrected himself.

The three days after Uncle Fred's accident were the loneliest days of my life. All I had left of Uncle Fred was a bunch of toys my dad didn't know how to play with.

And the house was so silent. My dad and I had nothing to talk about, so we just didn't speak.

Worst of all, I couldn't sleep. Every night that horrible dream came back—the dream about the statue in the graveyard.

Finally the minister looked up and asked, "Does anyone have anything they'd like to add?"

Dad patted me on the shoulder. "Danny?" he said.

I held up Uncle Fred's Red Baron Hot Wheels car. It had always been his favorite.

Uncle Fred was only the second person I'd ever known who'd died. The first was Grandma Walker, when I was little. And Uncle Fred was the only person who'd ever died right in front of me.

I set the car at the top of the plastic Hot Wheels track I had set up. The track looped and curved around the freshly dug dirt, ending in a final jump onto Uncle Fred's coffin.

Blinking back tears, I let the Red Baron go. It whizzed down the slope, streaked through the loop-the-loop, and flew off the last jump into the grave.

It landed with a tiny *ka-tink* on the top of the coffin. I knew Uncle Fred would have loved it.

I wiped my eyes. The funeral was officially over.

Most of the crowd scattered, heading off to their cars. But Coach Kankel stepped up to the grave and stared down at the coffin.

"Such a waste," he said. "Such a terrible, avoidable waste. . . ."

Taylor Morgan stood beside him and joked, "Don't be so hard on yourself, Coach. You must have *some* redeeming qualities."

He scowled at her. She turned to me and Dad. "I'm so sorry, Danny, James. If there's anything I can do, please let me know."

"Thanks, Taylor," Dad said. "Thanks very much."

"It's a little late for a nurse, don't you think?" Coach Kankel snapped, glancing at Uncle Fred's coffin.

"It won't be if I break your nose," she shot back. She gave me a small, sad smile and walked away to her car.

I wandered off, leaving Dad staring into the

grave. "Danny?" he called after me, but I kept walking. I found a bench at the edge of the cemetery and sat down on it. From there I could see the river in the distance. The afternoon sun sparkled on the water.

"I remember when my grandparents died," a voice behind me said.

I looked up to see Dayna Stenson standing nearby. She sat down beside me. "At first it doesn't seem real," she said. "And then, when it finally hits you that they're really dead, you start thinking about all the gross stuff that's happening to their bodies—down there. . . ."

She pointed to the ground. I blinked at her.

"If you don't mind, I'm still at the 'It doesn't seem real' part," I told her. "But thanks for the cheery thought."

"It *is* cheery," Dayna insisted. "When you think about it—"

"I'd rather not," I interrupted her. I hated the thought of Uncle Fred's body . . . the worms . . . I shuddered. I didn't want to think about it anymore.

But Dayna did.

"I mean the dying part is sad and scary, just because you can't do anything about it," she said. "But what comes next? It's like—a miracle in reverse. The cells breaking down, the flesh disintegrating, everything dissolving away . . . until all that's left is the space you filled in someone's heart."

I stared at her, stunned. I had never met a girl like her in my life. She was . . . totally deep.

"Aren't you a cheerleader?" I asked.

She smiled and gave me her hand. "Come with me," she said.

We walked out the cemetery gates and down the street. "Where are we going?" I asked her.

"You'll see," she said.

She walked down Elm and stopped in front of the old, abandoned Victorian house. The one I'd passed the other day on my way home from school. It was set back away from the street, and the tall trees cast so much shadow over it it seemed to be dark even on a sunny day like today.

I stared at the house, a nervous feeling growing in my stomach. "What is this place?" I asked her.

Dayna smiled mysteriously at me. The grass around the house had grown so tall that it hid any walkway or path there once might have been to the door. Dayna led me forward, trampling her way through the grass.

She stopped and swept the grass away from a rusty mailbox. When I read the name on the mailbox, my jaw dropped.

The only thing that kept me from running away then and there was Dayna's hand on mine.

The name on the mailbox was DANKO.

"You know who Curtis Danko is, right?" Dayna asked.

The creepy house loomed over me. "You mean the most *toasted* sculptor in Walker Falls?" I wisecracked.

"Don't make jokes," Dayna warned.

"Why not?" I asked.

"He might hear you," she answered, starting toward the house.

"Excuse me?" I called after her. I stayed right where I was. I liked Dayna a lot, but she was beginning to sound a little bit nuts. Just like everyone else in this town.

She paused at the front door and turned to face me. "Don't you want to see what's inside?"

The late afternoon light was fading fast.

"Well, you know . . ." I didn't want to look like a chicken in front of Dayna—but I didn't want to go into that house, either. "It's getting dark and . . ."

Dayna crouched down and fumbled in the brush near the door. A second later she stood up holding the ends of two extension cords in each hand. "Witness the miracle of modern technology," she said. She plugged the two ends into each other. Suddenly a pencil-thin beam of orange light glowed through the rusty keyhole of the door.

"Come on," Dayna said. "I put the lights on inside." She placed her hand on the knob and turned it. The front door opened with a creak. I crept up behind her, hesitating at the threshold. She dragged me inside and shut the door behind me.

"Whoa," I gasped. The house looked like the setting for the coolest Halloween party ever. The walls and doors were painted in spooky glow-in-the-dark orange and purple. Rows of electric jack-o'-lanterns glowed along the floor, and the corners were hung with fake cobwebs and strings of pumpkin lights. There were big Styrofoam tombstones, plastic cauldrons filled with fake arms and legs, and shrunken heads hanging in every doorway.

A plastic skeleton wore baggy clothes and a bushy black wig to make him look like Curtis Danko. He stood at the foot of the stairs, pointing the way up, past old portraits with the eyes cut out and big, scary glass eyes peeking through the holes. At the top of the stairs hung a candelabra with flickering flame light bulbs.

"What *is* this place?" I asked.

"It's a haunted house," Dayna replied. "The best haunted house ever!"

She threw open a closet door and shouted, "BOO!" A figured lurched out of the closet at me.

"Curtis Danko!" I screamed.

Dayna laughed. It was only a papier-mâché Curtis Danko. It wore another bushy-haired wig and a T-shirt with CURTIS DANKO written on it in Day-Glo letters.

"Where did you get all this stuff?" I asked. I'd never seen anything like it.

"People's attics and basements," she said. "Storage sheds, even car trunks."

"How did you manage to get it all here?" The people of Walker Falls couldn't even stand to hear the word *Halloween*. If they saw this, most of them would die of terror.

"I didn't," Dayna replied. "It came to me. Hidden in book bags, lunchboxes, clarinet cases. . . . All summer long, kids have been sneaking out after dinner to help me build this. They've been saving up all the candy their parents gave them, and they've been making costumes in secret. On Halloween night we're all going to trick or treat in here."

"But aren't you afraid of the curse of Curtis Danko?" I asked.

"Yes and no," Dayna said. "The whole Danko thing happened before we were born. And with Curtis locked up in his crypt and Halloween all put away and forgotten . . . we feel pretty safe. But we don't *want* to feel safe. We want to be just a little bit scared. Even if it's just for one night. Because it's fun!"

This is the coolest girl in the whole world, I thought as I stared at Dayna's creation.

"The kids of Walker Falls want their Halloween back," she said. "And tomorrow night I'm going to give it to them."

"Maybe—" a voice behind us said. Dayna and I whirled around to see Ryan and Leo, grinning in the doorway.

"And maybe not," Ryan finished. Something silvery flashed as he twirled it around his finger. It was a chain, and at the end of it hung the key to Curtis Danko's crypt.

"What are you doing here?" Dayna demanded.

Ryan twirled the key on its chain around his finger, back and forth, grinning like someone who has a secret. "What am *I* doing here? The question is, what are *you* doing here—on private property—*trespassing*?"

Dayna glared at him. What could she say? She *was* trespassing. But I was pretty sure no one cared about it—no one except Ryan.

"I've been watching you, Dayna," Ryan said. "Ever since Kelly Staranowicz first told me you were poking around in here. See, people tell you things—when you're popular."

He sneered at me as if to say that I *wasn't* popular.

"Or when you're a bully," Dayna snapped.

"Bully? Me?" Ryan walked across the foyer toward us, his eyes trained on me. "You've got me all wrong, Dayna. Just ask Danny. I'm not a bully, am I, Danny?"

He stopped right in front of me, his face only inches away from mine. Leo backed him up, snickering.

"Wuh . . . uh . . . no," I stammered. "I mean . . ."

"He's not going to do anything to us," Dayna said calmly. "And he can't make us do anything if we don't want to."

I wished I felt as sure of that as she did.

"Oh, really?" Ryan said. "Hmm. Let's do the math. My mom is the cheerleading coach . . . and you're a cheerleader, aren't you, Dayna?"

Dayna folded her arms across her chest. "So?"

"And my dad is the head coach *and* the assistant principal at school. That means he can make your lives torture if he wants to. He's also going to be mayor in a few days. And that means he gets to decide who gets a permit to open a candy factory—and who *doesn't*."

I felt my face turn red. That was it! Ryan was threatening me, Dayna, *and* my dad. I had heard enough.

I stepped toward him. "Okay, Ryan . . . we give up—"

"*What?*" Dayna glared at me.

"Hey, nobody ever died in a war by keeping his head down," I mumbled my explanation.

It was the way I'd always gotten through life—don't fight the bullies.

"Nobody ever *won* a war that way, either," Dayna snapped.

Ryan's key spun round and round on his finger, nearly hypnotizing me.

"What do you want?" I asked him.

"I want the room at the top of the stairs," he replied.

"No way!" Dayna cried. "We're going to have dancing in there."

"Trust me, Dayna," Ryan said. "I've got something much more fun to put up there."

He caught the key and dropped it into his pocket, staring into my eyes the whole time. Then he spun around on one heel and walked out the door. Leo followed him.

I let out a deep breath. "That was close."

"Yeah," Dayna said. "Close to the most cowardly thing I have ever seen! After what happened to your grandfather—I'd think you of all people would want to fight for Halloween."

She bolted out the front door and slammed it shut behind her.

I wanted to follow her—but then what? What could I say to defend myself? I was a coward—and there was nothing I could do about it.

I stood alone in the foyer of the haunted house,

staring at all the blinking lights and goofy decorations. At that moment it didn't feel like a party house at all. It just seemed . . . sad.

Suddenly everything went pitch black. "Hey!" I cried. "Who cut off the lights?"

I tried not to run. I knew it was probably just Ryan or maybe even Dayna, trying to scare me. I stood my ground for a few seconds, staring around the haunted house. "Hello?" I called. "Is anybody out there?"

Then, near the stairs, something glowed. I walked toward it. All the power had been cut—what could be glowing without electricity?

The glow came from one of the portraits by the stairs. I stepped closer—and screamed.

The portrait's eyes were glowing bright green!

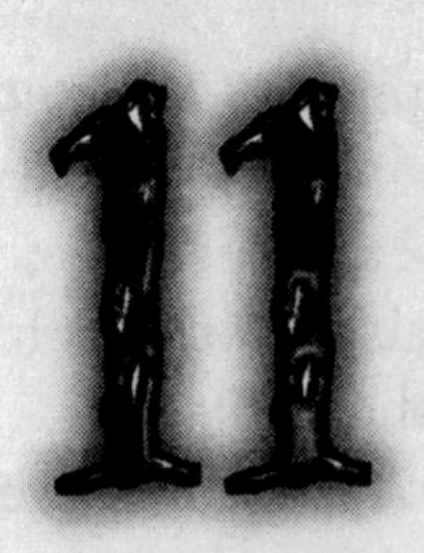

I ran out of the house as fast as I could. When I reached the street, I glanced back. No movement inside, no sign of life—nothing gruesome or hideous was chasing after me.

It must have been some kind of trick, I told myself. Glow-in-the-dark paint on the eyeballs or something. But the house was covered with glow-in-the-dark paint, and none of it glowed like those two greenish-yellow eyes.

They'd even flickered, kind of like fireflies.

The next morning was Halloween. I went to school for the first time since Uncle Fred's accident. When Mrs. Moore pulled up in her minivan, I climbed inside. Everyone stared at me, as usual. Only this time the other kids looked a little less mean. Not so much like they hated me. More like they just felt sorry for me now. I guess it was progress. But I still felt like an alien.

I gazed out the window as we drove to school so I wouldn't have to meet all those stares. The same old boring scenery went past as we whizzed up the street. I recognized the black iron cemetery fence and scanned it with my eyes without really looking.

Then something strange caught my eye. I sat up straight and plastered my face to the window, trying to see better.

"Stop the car!" I shrieked to Mrs. Moore. "Stop the car *now*!"

Mrs. Moore slammed on the brakes. The minivan squealed to a stop.

We had just passed Uncle Fred's freshly dug grave. And through the cemetery fence, I had seen tiny green lights blinking around his tombstone.

Fireflies!

"Back up! Back up!" I ordered.

"What is it, Danny?" Mrs. Moore asked. All the kids in the van stared at me as if I were crazy.

"There were fireflies!" I cried. "Over Uncle Fred's grave! Didn't you see it? Fireflies—in *October*!"

Mrs. Moore gave me a worried frown.

"I can prove it to you!" I shouted. "I can show you! Just back the car up!"

The minivan drove a few yards in reverse until I said, "Stop!" I stared through the cemetery fence. There was Uncle Fred's grave.

But the fireflies were gone.

• • •

"Danny?" Taylor Morgan looked worried as she studied my face.

Mrs. Moore had dragged me to the nurse's office as soon as we got to school. I insisted that I felt fine, but she wouldn't listen.

When Taylor heard what had happened, she called my dad at work and told him he'd better come in. Now he was sitting in her office with me, looking guilty.

"It always helps to talk about things that are bothering you," Taylor said.

"It doesn't help if people think you're nuts afterward," I pointed out.

"I'm sorry, Danny," Dad said. "I know you miss Uncle Fred. I miss him, too."

"Why?" I demanded. "What do you miss about him? His crazy costumes? His toys scattered all over the house? His wacky recipes? Do you miss him acting out stories for you, or helping you with your homework, or building models or playing slot cars, or sharing his space-food sticks with you, or offering to take you to see a space shuttle launch?"

Dad's face looked blank. He had no idea I was so close to Uncle Fred. I could see the shock in his eyes.

"Did you even know who he really was?" I asked him.

Dad's eyes grew damp as he blinked back tears. "Space-food sticks . . ." he murmured.

"You stuffed your dad's car trunk full of them, hoping he'd take you to Cape Kennedy—remember?" Taylor said.

I stared at her, surprised. How did she know that?

Dad checked his watch. "I have to go," he muttered.

"Maybe you should take Danny home early today," Taylor suggested. "Keep him out of school for a few more days."

Dad glanced at me, and then down at the floor. "You don't understand. I've got German investors coming. I've got a factory to decorate, all by myself, and then a four-hour round-trip drive to the airport—"

"Send a cab," Taylor said.

"Find me one with leather seats and a cell phone and we can talk," Dad told her.

I slumped in my seat. Dad was too busy, as usual. There was always something going on that was more important than me.

"Spend some time with him, James," Taylor urged him.

"I will," Dad promised. "Just as soon as Halloween is over."

Taylor leaned forward and looked Dad right in

the eye. "James. There are garbage trucks and volunteers walking up and down every street in Walker Falls yanking down your Spooktacular decorations. I'd say Halloween *is* over."

Dad shook his head. He wouldn't give up.

I couldn't take any more of this. I jumped out of my chair and bolted from the room.

"Danny—wait!" Taylor called after me.

I ran. I ran right out of school and didn't stop until I reached the street. Then I stuffed my hands in my pockets, hung my head, and started walking home.

Taylor was right. Up and down the street people were frantically tearing down the Halloween decorations Dad had put up. The grown-ups glared at me as I passed, but the little kids looked at me sort of hopelessly—as if they wanted to keep the decorations up and wished I could help them.

But what could I do? What could one kid do against a town full of nut-jobs?

Behind me I heard a loudspeaker. I turned to see Coach Kankel's Campaign Mobile approaching. The Campaign Mobile was a truck painted red, white, and blue with KANKEL FOR MAYOR signs all over it and a loudspeaker attached to the front. Coach Kankel drove it, shouting through the loudspeaker.

"TONIGHT IS HALLO-YOU-KNOW-WHAT!" he announced. "ONLY A FEW HOURS LEFT UNTIL

SUNDOWN. REMEMBER! THE ONLY SAFE HOUSE IS AN UNDECORATED HOUSE!"

I stared as the truck slowly rolled past. I hope he doesn't win the election, I thought. Mayor Churney is a jerk, but Coach Kankel is even worse!

"ONE PUMPKIN, ONE STYROFOAM TOMBSTONE, ONE LITTLE SHRED OF ORANGE OR BLACK CREPE PAPER COULD SPELL DISASTER FOR US ALL!" Coach Kankel cried. "THIS HALLOWEEN DECORATION REMOVAL SERVICE PAID FOR BY THE COMMITTEE TO ELECT KANKEL FOR MAYOR. DON'T FORGET OUR SILENT AUCTION FUND-RAISER AND OCTOBERFEST THIS AFTERNOON. THERE WILL BE PLENTY OF FOOD, AND CHEESY THE CLOWN WILL BE THERE FOR THE KIDS—"

"Cheesy the Clown?" I muttered. "Great. I'll be sure to miss it."

The Campaign Mobile turned a corner and rolled away down another street. I was glad to get away from it. I scowled and shuffled up the front walk of my house—the only house still decorated for Halloween.

I heard a familiar whizzing noise—*clack-zzzzz.* I looked down. A tiny Hot Wheels car rolled to a stop at my feet.

Where had that come from? I glanced at the front door. I saw another little car. This one flew out of the mail slot and whizzed down the front walk. I bent over to pick it up.

It was Uncle Fred's favorite car—the Red Baron.

I gasped when I remembered—the Red Baron? It couldn't be! I had buried the Red Baron in Uncle Fred's grave!

Clutching the little red car in my fist, I walked slowly toward the front door. Someone is playing a joke on me, I thought. An absolutely, totally cruel joke. But who?

I opened the front door and stepped inside. I didn't see anyone in the house. I leaned against the banister and I looked upstairs. "Hello?" I called.

Tick, tock, tick, tock . . .

The only sound I heard was the ticking of the grandfather clock at the top of the stairs. My heart seemed to pound in rhythm with the clock, *thump, thump, thump, thump. . . .*

I walked quietly to the kitchen. There, on the table, stood Uncle Fred's space shuttle model. He hadn't managed to finish it before he died.

But now—there it was. Gleaming. Completely finished and painted.

Who could have done that?

I glanced over my shoulder, all around the room. What was going on here?

"H-h-hello?" I whispered.

Whoosh! Out of the corner of my eye a shadow flashed past the kitchen door. I spun around—nothing. I slowly backed up against the sliding glass doors that led to the patio. The curtains on the doors were closed.

Light! I thought. A little extra light would be very good right now.

I fumbled for the string that pulled the curtains open, and heard a tiny sound behind me—*crunch, crunch, crunch.*

I whirled around and shrieked.

Uncle Fred stood in front of me—back from the grave!

"AAAAAAAH!" I screamed. I fell against the curtains, parting them. Light suddenly flooded the room.

"GLAAAAARRRRR!" Uncle Fred shrieked, dropping the box of cereal he had been holding. Uncle Fred covered his eyes, as if they weren't used to the light.

He peeked out at me from behind his hand. "Oh, it's *you*," he said.

I stopped screaming and stared at him. My heart pounded against my rib cage as if it wanted to break free. Calm down, I told myself. It's only Uncle Fred.

Then I realized—what was I thinking? "AAAAA-AAAAH!" I screamed again.

"Whoa!" Uncle Fred shouted. "Danny—it's okay. It's OKAY!"

I stopped screaming again. Uncle Fred grinned at me.

"B-b-b-but—you're—d-d-dead!" I stammered.

"Apparently not," Uncle Fred replied. "Though I did nearly kill myself when I looked in the mirror today. I mean, come on. A *tie*? What were you trying to do to me?"

This can't be happening, I thought. He's back—and he seems exactly the same! But that's totally impossible.

"I saw you," I said. "At the funeral home! You weren't moving at all. You weren't even *breathing*."

"Well, sure, it looked that way," Uncle Fred said. "I mean, *you* try breathing in a vest you haven't worn since your senior prom. I must've gotten just enough oxygen through my skin to keep me alive. That happens, you know—your skin actually breathes."

My heartbeat slowed down a little. All this talk of breathing reminded me I'd better do a little of it myself. I took a long, deep breath and tried to calm down.

"Okay," I said, staring hard at Uncle Fred. "That makes sense, I guess. So, what happened? I mean, how—?"

Uncle Fred sat down on the floor beside me. "Well, I got beaned by a pumpkin and out went the lights," he said. "The next thing I knew, I woke up in a box, six feet under."

I gasped. It sounded horrible. "What did you do?"

"I pretty much screamed my lungs out. And all

Here's Uncle Fred standing outside our house in Walker Falls.

Uncle Fred's favorite holiday was Halloween. He liked to play spooky jokes on people in town. Most of them thought he was spookier than his jokes.

But I knew he was a great guy—and the coolest grandpa anyone could ask for.

Things were pretty boring in Walker Falls—
until evil zombies rose from their graves!

Me, my friend Dayna, and our parents were totally scared! What did the zombies want? We didn't know, but it couldn't be good!

Then Uncle Fred lost his hand . . .

. . . and his legs and some arms. . .

. . . and we realized that he was a zombie, too!

But Uncle Fred was a good ghoul, not a bad one. We put him back together so he could help fight the evil zombies.

of a sudden there's this scratching sound on the outside of the coffin—and *bang!* Something breaks through the wood. I hear voices, and hands are pulling me out—"

"Who was it?" I asked.

"I don't know," Uncle Fred said. "It was still dark. I couldn't see their faces. And to be honest with you, I was in too much of a hurry to get out of there to stop and chat."

"Does Dad know about this yet?" I asked.

"Sure. I called him on his cell phone and said, 'Hi! It's your not-so-dead father calling from THE GRAVE!'" He rolled his eyes at me as if he'd never heard such a silly question. "Of course he doesn't know yet! I haven't figured out how to break the news to him."

I gazed at Uncle Fred. "I think Dad will be really happy to see you," I said.

Uncle Fred grinned. "Well, I think I can milk this almost-dead thing for at least a month's worth of sympathy, don't you?"

"Yeah," I replied. "At least."

He stood up and brushed himself off. "It's good to be back," he told me.

"It's good to have you back," I said, steadying myself. Uncle Fred folded me into a big bear hug, pressing my head against his chest. I was so happy he was still alive!

But I noticed something strange as I stood there with my ear pressed against him. Something was missing. In a flash I realized what it was.

A heartbeat.

I listened harder, but there was nothing. I grabbed his wrist. No sign of a pulse or anything. I pulled out of the hug and stared at him.

Okay, I thought. If Uncle Fred has no heartbeat, that means that he's dead. But if he's *walking around the house* with no heartbeat . . . wouldn't that mean that Uncle Fred is, technically, *un*-dead?

I swallowed hard.

Uncle Fred glanced at the clock on the wall and cried, "Whoa! It's seven-fifteen! I've got to run—"

"Run? Um, Uncle Fred, maybe you'd be better off lying down," I suggested.

"Are you kidding?" he said. "I've had enough lying down, thank you very much. I've got to hit the road!"

"The road?" I asked. "You just crawled out of the grave, and you want to go on a road trip?"

"Well, yeah. I mean, I just got a new lease on life. I can't waste it!" Uncle Fred exclaimed.

"But—what if it's not so much a lease as a rental?" I stepped in front of him, trying to keep him from leaving. "I mean, what if . . . you know . . . maybe you're not as okay as you think you are?"

He stepped around me and headed for the front

door. "I'm fine! In fact, I never felt better. Don't worry." He paused for a second and put a hand on my shoulder. "Hey, I don't have time to leave a note for your dad, so do me a favor and bring him up to speed on this, okay?"

He reached for the door. I threw myself in front of him and blocked the door with my body.

"Wait!" I cried. "Some people might, you know, *freak* if they saw a guy walking around whose funeral they just went to yesterday."

"Really?" Uncle Fred stared out the window at the neighbors tearing down the last of the Halloween decorations. A sly grin spread across his face. "Let's find out!"

Before I could stop him, he yanked open the door and stepped outside. "Uncle Fred—wait!" I shouted, following him.

The Kankel Campaign Mobile was rolling down the street toward our house. People gathered up garbage bags full of Halloween decorations and dumped them into the back of the truck. Ryan and his buddy Leo were standing in our front yard, yanking down a bed-sheet ghost from our old elm tree.

Uncle Fred stomped down the front steps. Ryan and Leo spotted him first. They froze in their tracks, their mouths hanging open.

"Kankel!" Uncle Fred yelled, stomping toward the truck.

The brakes squealed as the truck came to a dead stop. Coach Kankel stared at Uncle Fred, his eyes bulging with fear.

"AAAAAH!" he screamed. Uncle Fred strode right up to him.

"Get those mouth-breathing kids off our lawn before I EAT THEIR NONEXISTENT BRAINS!" Uncle Fred shouted.

Ryan and Leo raced for the Campaign Mobile. They ran around to the passenger side and dived into the backseat of the cab.

Coach Kankel just gaped at Uncle Fred, too stunned to move.

"Something wrong with your jaw muscles, Coach?" Uncle Fred said. "They're usually in such good shape!"

"Y-y-y-you're dead!" Coach Kankel stammered.

"You're right!" Uncle Fred snapped. "Or at least I was! And I was resting pretty darn comfy, too, until I sensed what you were up to."

Coach Kankel's normally red face turned white. "S-s-s-sensed?"

"There are worlds beyond this world, Kankel," Uncle Fred told him. "Times beyond this time—as you will soon find out!"

He thrust his arm through the open window and grabbed for Coach Kankel's throat. Ryan and Leo screamed.

"Get away from me!" Coach Kankel shouted. He slid to the other side of the cab, locking the door and trying to kick Uncle Fred away with his feet.

"Not a chance, pal," Uncle Fred said, still trying to grab Coach Kankel. "I didn't dig my way out of the ground just to let you get away with this. I returned here to get you—and take you back to the grave with me!"

He finally got a grip on Coach Kankel's collar and yanked the coach's face close to his own. The boys huddled in the backseat, shaking with fright.

"Let's go!" Uncle Fred yelled.

"Uncle Fred!" I cried. "What are you doing?"

Coach Kankel stabbed desperately at the window button. With a whir the window slowly slid up.

"Come on, come on," Coach Kankel muttered at the window. "Close faster!"

Uncle Fred kept his grip on Coach Kankel's collar, his hand just inside the truck cab. The window rolled up almost to the top of the truck door. It hit Uncle Fred's wrist and slowed down.

"Uncle Fred!" I screamed. "Your hand!"

With a *shklump*, the window closed all the way—slicing Uncle Fred's hand off at the wrist!

The hand dropped inside the truck cab, but it kept its grip on Coach Kankel's shirt. Coach Kankel screamed and tried to shake the hand off without touching it. It finally flew into the backseat, landing on Ryan's lap.

Ryan and Leo shrieked with horror. Ryan batted the hand away. But the hand leaped up and slapped Leo across the face. Then it jumped back into the front seat.

I gasped. It was as if the hand had a mind of its own!

Coach Kankel yelped with terror and stepped on the gas. *Screech!* The Campaign Mobile peeled out, roaring off down the street.

Uncle Fred stared at his stumpy, handless arm. Some neighbors had heard the commotion and gathered around. Their mouths hung open as they gaped at Uncle Fred, shocked.

"Anybody else want a piece of me?" Uncle Fred shouted.

As if waking from a coma, the neighbors snapped out of it and ran as fast as they could to their own houses, slamming their doors behind them.

Uncle Fred turned back toward the house—and spotted me staring at the place where his hand used to be. I was shaking, and he must have seen the terror on my face. But he only blinked at his dry, bloodless stump.

"It's not so bad," he said. "Look, it's not even bleeding."

Is he *crazy*? I wondered. "Uncle Fred," I said. "You lost your hand."

He sighed. "Good thing my car's an automatic."

I shook my head. "Uncle Fred, listen to me." I had to get through to him. "Your hand is heading west on Mulberry Street at sixty miles per hour."

Uncle Fred walked over to where his old car sat in the driveway, covered with a dirty old tarp. He hadn't driven it in years. I'd never even seen it. He yanked the tarp off. It was a gleaming Ford Edsel, black, very old, in perfect condition.

Uncle Fred opened the door. "Well, then," he said. "I'd better go pick up my hand. Maybe you could call Mrs. Kankel and ask her to put it on ice for me until I can get over there. Okay? See ya!"

He climbed into the car, started it, and hit the gas. The Edsel zoomed out of the driveway and down the street, leaving me in its dust. I stared after it, blinking, totally confused.

What was going on with Uncle Fred?

How could he be dead one day, and un-dead the next?

And what about his hand?

I shuddered. How could it be? What was going on here?

I had no clue—but I had an idea about who might help me find out . . . Dayna Stenson.

I looked up her address in the school directory—811 Elm Lane. It was on the way to school, about half a mile from my house. I walked over there and spotted Curtis Danko's house not far off. I rubbed my sweaty hand on my jeans and rang the doorbell.

The door opened—and there stood Taylor Morgan.

"Taylor!" I gasped. I hadn't expected to see her.

"Hello, Danny." She smiled at me. "What a nice surprise."

"What are *you* doing here?" I asked.

"Well—I *live* here," she replied.

She lived there? "You mean you're Dayna's mother?" I had never thought of it before because they had different last names.

Taylor nodded toward the stairs. "Dayna's in her room."

I bounded up the stairs and entered Dayna's room. "Dayna?" I called. There was no one there. Where was she?

I was about to leave when I noticed an extension cord leading from a wall outlet, across the floor, and out the window. From there the cord snaked across the yard into Curtis Danko's house.

She must be over there, I thought, hurrying out of the house. I raced across the yard and burst into Curtis Danko's house. Dayna was rushing around putting up last-minute Halloween decorations. She didn't notice me until I nearly bumped into her.

"AAAAH!" she shouted, jumping with surprise. Then she scowled and said, "What do *you* want?"

"Dayna, I'm sorry I didn't stick up for you before," I began, hurrying to get in as many words as I could before I lost her attention. "But I have something really weird to tell you and I need you to just listen and not think I'm crazy, even though I may be, but I don't think I am—"

"Does it involve fireflies in the graveyard?" she asked, glaring at me.

"Actually, it involves other things . . . *out* of the graveyard," I said carefully. I didn't want to break it to her too quickly.

"Like what other things?" she asked, frowning.

"Like, oh, say . . ." I paused. She's going to think I'm completely nuts, I thought. But here goes. "Like my Uncle Fred?"

Nothing on her face moved, except for her eyelids. They blinked. Twice.

"You said we all want to be a little scared," I began.

Taylor's voice interrupted me. "Dayna?" she called. I jumped. Where had that come from?

Dayna hurried to an intercom plugged into a wall socket. She pushed Talk and said, "Yes?" She released the button and explained, "I have another intercom set up in my room. That way Mom thinks I'm up there when I'm really over here."

Clever, I thought, admiring her. Beauty *and* brains.

"I have to go to this Kankel for Mayor nightmare," Taylor's voice said. "Do you guys want to come?"

Dayna began to say, "No, thank you," but I cut her off and shouted, "We'd love to!"

Dayna glared at me.

"Trust me, okay?" I whispered. I had a feeling I knew where I could find Uncle Fred.

She scowled at me. "If I miss my own Halloween party because of this, the name Walker Falls is going to have a whole new meaning," she warned. "Because you are in for a *big* fall."

I gulped. I didn't think she was kidding.

• • •

The Kankels' huge backyard was decorated to look like an Alpine village for the Octoberfest. A brass band played oompah music on a bandstand near the big house. Mr. Kankel looked uncomfortable, dressed in those weird green suede German shorts with suspenders and a matching cap with a feather. Mrs. Kankel wore a long dress and a helmet with horns on top, like an opera singer. She was running the silent auction. I scanned the tables to see what was for sale. Most of it was junky handicrafts.

Mrs. Kankel stood with a microphone in front of a small crowd of townspeople, holding up a painting of a cat crying, done on black velvet.

"This finely crafted weeping kitty-cat painting might sell for thousands of dollars in stores," she said. I couldn't imagine what stores she was thinking of. I wouldn't pay two cents for that thing. "What will you generous folks bid for it?"

The crowd just stared at her. No one bid on the painting. Then, from the back of the crowd, someone shouted, "How are we supposed to bid on anything? We're unemployed!"

Coach Kankel piped up, "Hey! This is a silent auction!" He checked his watch and muttered, "Where's that stupid clown?"

"Come on, you two," Taylor said to Dayna and

me. "Let's check out the kiddie section."

We wandered to another part of the yard. A small stage was set up there for Cheesy the Clown. A bunch of little kids sat at some picnic tables, banging their mugs and screaming, "We want Cheesy! We want Cheesy!"

We sat down at an empty picnic table. Dayna was seething with anger. She obviously didn't want to be there. Nobody in their right mind would want to be. But I just knew Uncle Fred would show up, and I told her so.

I had tried to explain the rest—about Uncle Fred rising from the dead and losing his hand and everything—before we met Taylor and drove over here. I was able to get all the big stuff in, at least.

"Well?" Dayna whispered as I glanced around the yard. "Where is he?"

"Keep your eyes out for a hand without a body," I whispered back. "If we find his hand, he won't be far behind."

"Oh. Sure," Dayna said, with a look of disbelief.

A hand gripped my shoulder from behind.

A cold hand.

Uncle Fred's hand! I jumped, then whirled around.

But the hand on my shoulder was attached to an arm—and not Uncle Fred's. It was Dad.

"Hey, Danny," he said.

"Dad! What are you doing here?" I asked.

"I'm taking the night off," he said. He smiled at Taylor. She smiled back. I began to wonder if something was going on between them. But I was more worried about what Dad would do when he saw Uncle Fred—un-dead.

"But—why?" I asked him. "Who's putting up decorations at the factory? Who's making the chocolate?"

"Who's meeting the Germans at the airport?" Taylor added.

"Mrs. Vanderspool is picking them up," Dad replied. "I figure since Halloween isn't going to happen, we might as well make the best of what we've got. And if our chocolate doesn't speak for itself, no amount of Halloween Spooktacularity is going to make the Germans invest their money. Besides, Danny, when was the last time you and I had a night out together?"

Oh, great, I thought. *Now* he wants to spend time with me? I didn't want Dad to see Uncle Fred—at least, not yet. "Dad! You've got work to do!" I cried. "You have to go to the factory. Go! Now!"

Dad stared at me, surprised. Then we both turned toward the roar of little kids as Coach Kankel shoved a tall, thin man in a clown suit and makeup onto the stage.

"Uh . . . hey, kids." The man waved shyly at the children. "I'm . . . Cheesy the Clown . . . I guess."

"Hi, Cheesy!" the kids yelled.

What a weird clown, I thought. He doesn't seem like he knows what he's doing.

Cheesy glanced at Coach Kankel, who folded his arms across his chest and scowled at him. The clown turned back toward the audience and asked, "Uh—who wants to see some magic?"

"We do!" the kids shouted.

The kids' excitement seemed to warm Cheesy up. He smiled, then walked over to me.

"Put 'er there, pal!" Cheesy said, shoving his hand at me. I shook my head. I didn't want to be part of this stupid clown's act.

"Go on, kid, shake," Cheesy insisted.

I could tell he wasn't going to leave me alone until I did what he wanted. I grabbed his hand—and it came off!

The kids laughed. I stared at the hand I was holding. It was rubber, not real. Then I studied the clown's face. He waggled his bushy gray eyebrows at me.

Uncle Fred! Uncle Fred was Cheesy the Clown!

I screamed and dropped the rubber hand in the grass.

"That's my boy," Dad said, patting me on the back. "I was always afraid of clowns, too."

"AAAAAAAH!" I kept screaming.

"What's wrong?" Dayna whispered to me.

Uncle Fred picked up the rubber hand off the grass. "I'll take that." He tossed the fake hand high in the air and caught it inside his big clown pants.

"That's my dead Uncle Fred!" I whispered to Dayna.

She frowned. "It's Cheesy the Clown!" she insisted.

"It's my dead Uncle Fred *dressed* as Cheesy the Clown," I told her.

"He doesn't look very dead to me," Dayna whispered.

"That's my point!" I cried.

"Okay, kids," Uncle Fred called. "Here's the

trick." He waved his stumpy arm at the kids. "My magic hand has disappeared—and I will need it back, if you want me to hand one of you this *hundred-dollar bill*!" In his one good hand he held up a hundred-dollar bill. "The first one to find my magic hand gets the money!"

The kids screamed with delight and leaped from their seats. They charged Uncle Fred, tackled him, and tried to rip his big clown pants off.

"No! No!" Uncle Fred shouted. "My magic hand is somewhere in the house!" He pointed to the back door of the Kankels' house. Coach Kankel was standing right in front of it.

The kids stampeded toward the house. Coach Kankel's face turned white as they ran toward him. "No!" he shrieked. "No! Nooooo!"

The army of kids knocked him over and ripped open the door. They charged inside the house. I could hear the sounds of glass breaking as the kids tore the house apart.

Taylor turned to me and Dayna. "Now aren't you two glad you came?"

"Come on, Dayna," I said, jumping to my feet. "Let's go find that hand."

We bolted to the house, following the mob of kids. We raced through the house, then out the front door.

"There it is!" I shouted to Dayna. I pointed to

Uncle Fred's hand, darting through the grass on its fingertips as if they were legs. Wrapped around one finger was a chain with a key dangling from the end.

Uncle Fred jumped in front of the hand and crouched down like a catcher. "There you are!" he called. "Come to Papa!"

Uncle Fred dived for the hand, but the hand dodged to the left. Uncle Fred missed and tumbled to the ground. A squad of screaming kids chased after the hand.

Dayna and I hurried up to Uncle Fred and helped him to his feet. "What are you doing?" I demanded. "Why are you making your hand run around like this?"

"It's not me!" Uncle Fred said. "I'm not controlling it!"

"Then who is?" Dayna asked.

Coach Kankel ran up to Uncle Fred and grabbed him by the arm. "YOU!" he shouted. "You're ruining my fund-raiser! Who are you working for—Mayor Churney?"

I grabbed Uncle Fred's other arm and cried, "Let him go!" I tugged on one arm. Coach Kankel tugged on the other arm.

Skrrriitch! Uncle Fred's eyes bulged out as both his arms snapped off like the ends of a wishbone!

"Make a wish!" Uncle Fred joked.

"AAAAAAAH!" Coach Kankel screamed. He dropped the arm and ran away.

Uncle Fred spotted his hand across the lawn, running from a mob of kids. "Hang on to my arms for me, Danny," he said. He raced, armless, after his missing hand. I scooped up the arm Coach Kankel had dropped.

"I can't believe I'm doing this." I shook my head.

The hand headed for the fence that bordered the Kankels' yard. "It's trying to get away!" Dayna shouted.

Uncle Fred charged after it, and slipped! He fell headfirst into a big, open musician's trunk that belonged to the drummer.

Crash! Uncle Fred landed hard, his legs hanging out of the trunk. Coach Kankel slammed down the trunk lid—and cut off Uncle Fred's legs!

"AAAAAAAAH!" Coach Kankel screamed as the legs dropped on the grass.

Dayna and I hurried over to the trunk, lugging the two arms. Dayna opened the trunk. I dropped the arms inside, and then the two legs. Now at least he had all his pieces in one place—except for his right hand.

"Hmmm," Uncle Fred said. "I'd hate to leave empty-handed."

"Come on, Uncle Fred," I said, closing him up in the trunk. He couldn't walk on his own—so Dayna and I would have to carry him.

We dragged the trunk across the grass. Dad and Taylor waved to us from across the yard. They looked as if they were having a good time together.

"Where are you two headed?" Taylor called.

"We're just helping the band pack up," Dayna lied, pointing to the drum trunk we were lugging.

"Yeah," I added. "Just giving them a hand."

"And an arm and a leg . . ." Uncle Fred joked from inside the trunk.

"Don't go too far," Dad called. "the German investors should be here soon. I'd like you to meet them."

"Okay, Dad." I smiled and nodded as if everything were perfectly normal.

We stumbled into the street. Dayna gasped, dropping her end of the trunk.

"Ouch!" Uncle Fred groaned.

I looked up. When I saw what Dayna was looking at, I dropped the trunk, too.

"Hey!" Uncle Fred yelped.

"Whoa—" I murmured in amazement.

"What?" Uncle Fred pounded on the trunk lid. "What's going on out there?"

The whole neighborhood was decorated for Halloween again—even more than before. Orange lights blinked from every house, and the doors and windows were papered with skeletons, ghosts, pumpkins, and orange and black streamers. An orange Volkswagen was even painted to look like a giant jack-o'-lantern.

"We just got here an hour or so ago, right?" I asked Dayna, still having trouble believing my eyes. "And none of this was here then—right?"

Dayna nodded. "Who did this?"

Uncle Fred banged on the trunk again. "What?" he demanded. "Who did what?"

"Someone decorated the whole neighborhood for Halloween again," I explained.

And then I had a terrible thought.

"Uncle Fred, remember when you told me someone busted you out of your coffin?" I asked.

"Yeah . . ." Uncle Fred replied.

"Was there a hole in the top of your grave?" I asked.

"Come to think of it, no—" Uncle Fred told me.

I started to shake. What I was thinking was crazy—but a lot of crazy things had happened today.

"That means—" I began, glancing nervously around as the afternoon began to fade into darkness. "Whoever freed you had to do it . . . from under the ground."

Dayna looked confused. Then her jaw began to quiver as she stared over my shoulder. I spun around.

Over the hill behind me the moon was beginning to rise, big, full, and yellow. And in front of the moon, stumbling down the street, was an army of ragged figures. They didn't look like normal people. Their legs moved as if they hadn't walked in a long time.

My heart began to pound.

"Zombies!" I cried.

Uncle Fred popped his head out of the trunk and stared down the street. "Zombies!" he yelled. "Well, those Germans are sure to get a great Halloween show now!"

"Let's get out of here!" I yelled, pushing Uncle Fred's head back inside the trunk.

Dayna and I hurried back to my house, lugging Uncle Fred and his parts the whole way. We dragged the trunk up the front steps. I glanced down the street—no sign of the zombies. Then we ran inside the house and locked the door behind us.

I opened the trunk lid. "Thanks," Uncle Fred said. "It was getting stuffy in there." He glanced at his unattached arms and legs. "Can I get a little help?" he asked.

I ran to Dad's tool bench in the garage and came back with some screws and a screwdriver. "Think this will work?" I asked Uncle Fred.

He nodded. "I don't see why not."

Dayna and I took him into the kitchen and settled his torso into Dad's rolling office chair. Dayna's face turned green as she queasily picked up one of Uncle Fred's arms and held it up to his shoulder. "I'll hold it in place," she said. "You attach it."

I screwed Uncle Fred's arm onto his shoulder. It seemed to hold.

"It's working," I said.

Uncle Fred swung his arm around. "Yes, that's much better. Now do the other arm."

Dayna and I screwed on his other arm, then his legs. "There," I said at last. "We're done."

Uncle Fred looked down and frowned. "Why are my shoes on the wrong feet?" he asked.

I grimaced. We'd mixed up his right and left legs. "Oops," I said.

Something tapped on the patio door. I turned around and peered through the glass. I looked left, looked right—no one there. Then I looked down.

It was Uncle Fred's missing hand! The hand waved to me. I slid open the door.

"It's for you," I told Uncle Fred. The hand scurried inside, still dragging the key on its chain. Uncle Fred snatched up the key and studied it.

"Nothing like having something hand-delivered to make you feel important!" he said.

I stared at the key. I knew I'd seen it somewhere

before. Ryan Kankel had been swinging it around his finger when he threatened to make me look at Curtis Danko's sculpture.

"That's the key to Curtis Danko's crypt," I told Uncle Fred.

Uncle Fred scolded his hand as if it were a bad puppy. "How did you get this? What did you do? What did you do?"

"Your hand must have stolen it from Ryan Kankel," I said. I unscrewed Uncle Fred's legs and began to reattach them the right way. "Ryan wanted to find out what Curtis Danko's statue looked like—but he was too chicken to look at it himself. So he wanted *me* to look at it, but I ran away. I wonder if he's done something with the statue?"

I stepped back to make sure I'd screwed the right leg to the right side and the left to the left. Uncle Fred admired his feet. "That's more like it!"

Outside I heard a car pull into the driveway. "That must be Dad," I said. I didn't want him to see Uncle Fred right away—it would be too much of a shock. So I dropped a big sheet over Uncle Fred's head. "Hey!" he cried.

"Wait here," I said to Dayna. I ran to the door and opened it just as Dad got out of the car. He was with Dayna's mom. The two of them hurried into the house.

"Dad—we have to talk," I said.

Dad and Taylor gawked at the living room,

which was—for the second time now—heavily decorated for Halloween.

"Who put all our decorations back up?" Dad asked.

I didn't know what to say, but I had to say something. "Dad?" I began, fumbling for words. "What if people who really loved Halloween—people like Uncle Fred, for example—what if they had, um, Halloween . . . *issues* . . . that weren't quite over when they died?"

I paused to check on Dad's reaction so far. He was staring at me with his mouth slightly open, waiting for me to make sense.

"Did you ever think," I went on, "that they might stick around to work through their issues by, say, oh, rising from the grave?"

There—I'd said it. Sort of. I watched Dad's face for signs of trauma. Then I glanced over at the sheet covering Uncle Fred.

"Uh, no. Not really," Dad said. He was still watching me with his mouth open.

At that moment, Uncle Fred peeked out from under the sheet. "Hi, son," he said to my dad.

Dad and Taylor wobbled on their feet, then they both collapsed to the floor in a faint.

"Hey—Walkers!" Our neighbor Roy Koogle suddenly appeared in our doorway, frantically waving his arms.

"Run for your lives!" he shouted. "They're everywhere!"

"Who?" I asked.

"*The zombies!*" Mr. Koogle shrieked. He ran off, shouting his warning to everyone he saw.

I ran to the front door, and saw zombies coming up the driveway. "No!" I gasped.

I sped to the back door. Zombies were climbing up the porch!

"They're everywhere!" I yelled. "There's no way out!"

Dayna rolled her eyes. "Why don't you call for help?" She handed me the phone.

"Good idea," I said. I took the receiver from her and started to dial. ***Click.***

The line went dead.

"Hello? Hello?" I shouted. Nothing.

I stared at the phone. "What's wrong?" Dayna asked.

"They've cut the phone lines," I told them.

"Who?" Dayna asked.

"The ZOMBIES!" I screamed.

Uncle Fred tried to calm me down. "Danny, it's okay. We're safe for now. There are no zombies in here."

"*You're* a zombie!" I cried, without realizing what I was saying. My breath caught in my throat for a moment. It was true. I had to face facts. Uncle Fred was a zombie!

"I mean besides me!" Uncle Fred said.

I thought I was losing my mind. "I don't understand this!" I shouted. "One minute you're alive and then you're dead and then you're alive again but you're still dead and suddenly there are hands and arms and legs and screwdrivers and—HOW DID THIS HAPPEN?"

Uncle Fred grabbed my shoulders and shook them lightly. "Danny, listen to me. You remember all those fireflies we tried to catch last summer? And how one day, when it started to turn cold, they just . . . didn't come back?"

I nodded.

"Well, what do you think happened to them?" Uncle Fred asked.

"They died, I guess," I said.

"Yes and no." Uncle Fred smiled at me. "When all those millions of fireflies die, their bodies come undone, but they release their magic glow into the ground. It just collects down there, waiting for someone to use it. I used the magic of the fireflies to come back here. Their glow contains some pretty powerful magic. If you can figure out how to use it, you can do just about anything. All you have to do is really, really want something with all your heart." He paused, as if he were a little choked up. "Like being back with the the people you love."

"Or the people you *hate*," Dayna put in.

Uncle Fred let go of my shoulders. "What do you mean?" I asked.

"If Uncle Fred can wish himself back, why couldn't Curtis Danko do the same thing?" Dayna explained. "And if he got loose, imagine what he might do."

We could hear the zombies outside the house, shuffling their feet and groaning loudly.

Bam! Bam! Bam! They banged on the door, trying to get inside!

I could smell them now. My nostrils filled with the stench of decaying flesh. I started to gag.

"Listen," Dayna said. "They're chanting, but I can't make out what they're saying."

Dayna was right. They were speaking, and as they drew closer, I could finally make out their words.

"Staaaatuuuuue," the zombies moaned. "STAAAAAA-TUUUUUE!"

"Oh, no!" I gasped. "They want Curtis Danko's statue! Someone must have taken it from the crypt!"

"What are we going to do?" Dayna cried.

"Staaaatuuuue," the zombies groaned. "Staaaa-tuuuue! Staaaatuuuue!"

"I think I know where the statue is," I said, thinking of Ryan Kankel. He had wanted to use a room in Curtis Danko's house. Maybe he wanted to put the statue in that room.

"Good," Uncle Fred said. "Curtis must want it badly—he raised the dead to get it! Maybe we can get to it first and use it as bait!"

"Bait?" Dayna asked. "For what?"

I knew what Uncle Fred meant. "To lure Curtis back to the grave."

"Exactly," Uncle Fred said. "Once he's in his crypt, we slam the door on him and lock the chain around it."

A zombie pressed his face against the window.

"Come on!" I shouted. "We've got to run!"

"Run?!" Uncle Fred said. "I can hardly walk! You guys go get Curtis Danko's statue and return it. I'll take care of these two." He gestured at Dad and Taylor, still out cold.

"What are you waiting for?" Uncle Fred yelled. "Go!"

I threw my arms around his neck and hugged him. Then Dayna and I ducked through a side window, out into the night.

All along the dark street, people were being chased by zombies. Dayna and I kept to the shadows. We sneaked down block after block until we came to the cemetery. "We've got to get to Curtis

Danko's house," I said. "And the fastest way is—" I paused. "Through the cemetery."

"I knew that," Dayna murmured.

We slipped through the bars of the cemetery fence, and the two off us took off, through the graveyard, on the night of the living dead!

The cemetery was quiet. “All of the zombies must be stalking the streets,” I whispered.

We crept through the maze of gravestones, holding our breath. Dayna stopped short and whispered, “Look!”

Just ahead was Curtis Danko’s crypt. The chain lay loosely on the ground. The door stood ajar. A faint greenish-yellow light glowed from inside the crypt.

Dayna clutched my hand.

“He’s out,” I said. “For sure.”

We ran through the cemetery as fast as we could. When we reached the other side, we slipped through the fence and hurried to Curtis Danko’s house.

I could hear a low pulse of music coming from inside the house. “The party’s already started,” Dayna said.

We sprinted up the steps to the front door. A tall kid dressed as an ape in some kind of armor stood alone on the porch. He was staring into the house through a crack in the wall. A shaft of light leaked through the crack.

"Hey," I asked him. "Have you seen Ryan Kankel?"

The ape warrior turned and stared at me and Dayna. He slowly shook his head no.

"Thanks," I said. I opened the front door and Dayna and I went inside.

The party was in full swing. Dayna had done an amazing job with the decorations—the house looked spooky but totally cool. Kids in costumes were dancing in the main foyer, hanging on the stairs, talking. Other kids were exploring the long, dark hallways. Whenever something scary popped out at them—a skeleton, a Curtis Danko head—they screamed and laughed.

I spotted Ryan and Leo standing in a corner of the main room. Ryan was watching the other kids with a mischievous grin on his face.

I crossed the room. "Ryan! Where's the statue?"

"You'll see," Ryan said. "Soon enough. Or not—depending on how much money you've got in your pocket."

"What are you talking about?" Dayna demanded.

"The statue," Ryan replied. "I'm going to force

kids to look at it—unless they pay me. If they don't want to go blind, they'll fork over the cash."

"Listen to me, Ryan," I said. "Curtis Danko is alive! When you stole his statue, you woke him up and made him mad. And now he's coming to get it back!"

Ryan laughed. "Man, you Walkers never give up, do you? You think I believe in all this zombie garbage? Do I look like an idiot to you?"

Boom! The front door burst open. A bunch of kids in costumes ran into the house screaming, "ZOMBIES! RUN! RUN!"

Behind them, a horde of growling, groaning zombies stomped in.

Ryan scowled. "Oh, yeah, right! Nice try! As if a *real* zombie would wear a rubber mask like this!"

Ryan reached out toward one of the zombies.

"Ryan—no!" I shouted. Too late.

Ryan ripped the zombie's face off. Underneath, a rotting skull grinned back at him.

"AAAAAAAAH!" Ryan screamed.

The zombie roared.

I grabbed Ryan's arm and ran. We ran with all the kids up the stairs and into a dark, empty room. We slammed the door shut against the zombies and threw our weight against it, hoping to keep the zombies out.

Bam! Bam! Bam! The zombies pounded their

fists on the door. We all screamed. *Smash!* A zombie fist crashed through the door, splintering the wood.

"Help!" a girl cried. "Somebody help us!" Kids backed from the door, huddling in the center of the room.

Smash! Another zombie fist burst through the door. Then another. More kids bolted away from the door.

But Dayna, Ryan, Leo, and I stayed. We pressed against the door with all our strength.

Then I noticed something glowing. I saw two fireflies zip through the door's keyhole. I watched them as they flew across the room. They flitted around the kids, then headed to a trick-or-treater who stood alone—the kid in the ape warrior costume.

The two fireflies hovered over him and settled in the eyeholes of his ape mask. They sat there and glowed—right where the kid's eyes should have been.

Everyone stared at that kid in the ape costume. He reached his hand to his face and slowly peeled the rubber mask away.

Underneath was nothing but a skull—a skull with bushy dark hair and two fireflies for eyes.

"No!" I gasped. "It's Curtis Danko!"

The walls shook with our screams.

"He's going to eat our brains!" Ryan yelped. "He's going to eat our BRAINS!"

The huddle of kids backed away from Curtis Danko.

Bam! The doors flew open and the zombies marched into the room.

Stomp. Stomp. Stomp.

The zombies moved toward us, and the floorboards beneath us began to groan.

Stomp. Stomp. Stomp.

The floorboards creaked.

I looked down at the moldy carpet beneath our feet.

A floorboard broke with a sickening snap.

Then another, and another.

"Nooo!" I screamed as we all plunged down to the floor below.

I landed with a thud on top of somebody, and somebody landed on top of me. I heard some kids moaning, but everyone seemed to be okay. Dayna stood slowly, brushing herself off.

I glanced around the room, searching for Curtis Danko, but I couldn't find him in the tangle of arms and legs.

What I did see was much worse.

The entire town—Mr. and Mrs. Kankel, the Churneys, Sheriff Frady, Dad, and Uncle Fred. They'd all been captured, just like us. The zombies had herded them into Curtis Danko's house. Taylor was propped up on a sofa, her head hanging back, still out cold.

"What do they want?" Mayor Churney babbled. Sweat poured down his face, even though the night was cool. "What do they *want?*"

"Probably human flesh!" Coach Kankel said.

Everyone stared at Mayor Churney's wife, who was very fat. If human flesh was what they wanted, Mrs. Churney could feed them all.

"This can't be happening!" Coach Kankel blurted. "But it is!"

"Will you make up your mind?" Mayor Churney cried. "Are we going to die or not?"

"No!" Coach Kankel sputtered. "I mean, yes! I mean, I don't know!"

"We're definitely going to die," Sheriff Frady said. "I have that kind of luck."

"I've got to get out of here! I've got to get out of here!" Coach Kankel shouted. With a football player's move, he broke through the line of zombies and ran out the door. Something told me he wouldn't get very far.

"Staaaatuuuuee," the zombies murmured.

I looked to the center of the room. An empty pedestal stood there. It had been meant for the town monument that was never erected.

A group of zombies was carrying something toward it. It was tall and covered in a canvas shroud. The crowd stepped back as the zombies passed through.

When they reached the pedestal, the zombies parted to make way for someone standing at the edge of the crowd.

"Oh, no," Uncle Fred murmured.

I saw a shock of messy black hair, and the skeleton face lighted by two firefly eyes. The crowd gasped. Curtis Danko had finally returned to seek his revenge.

Standing tall, Curtis Danko strode toward the pedestal in the center of the room. The covered statue stood on top of it, tied with rope.

Curtis's glowing eyes seemed to burn through everyone he looked at.

"What does he want?" Mrs. Churney whispered.

"He wants to show us what's under that shroud!" Ryan cried. "He wants to burn our eyes out and make our heads explode and—"

"We're all going to die!" Mayor Churney sobbed. "We're all going to die! I'm not going to get reelected, and we're all going to die!"

Dayna tapped me on the shoulder. "Look!" she said. "Mom's finally waking up!"

I turned to see Taylor open her eyes and shake her head. She glanced at the scene around her—the whole town huddled in Curtis Danko's house, surrounded by zombies. Then she spotted Curtis Danko standing by the pedestal.

Her neck suddenly went limp. Her head lolled back on the sofa. She passed out again.

Curtis stepped in front of the pedestal and raised his arms.

"Wait!" a voice called out. It was Dad.

Dad struggled through the crowd and made his way to Curtis. "Please," Dad said. "Don't hurt them. It's not their fault. If I hadn't wanted to be a hero so badly—"

"Yeah!" Ryan shouted. "It's his fault!"

"No!" Dayna cried. "It's my fault! I'm the one who talked all the other kids into celebrating Halloween!"

"Yeah!" Ryan shouted again. "It's her fault!"

"No!" I called to Curtis. "It's *my* fault! I knew Ryan broke into your crypt and stole your statue, but I was too afraid to stand up to him or tell anyone!"

"Yeah!" Ryan said. "You coward!"

The whole town glared at Ryan—including Curtis Danko.

Ryan shrank back. "Come on!" he sputtered. "It—it was just a joke."

"EEEEEYYYYYAAAAHHH!" A war cry echoed in my ears. Everyone turned to the front door. Coach Kankel charged in, wearing his old high school football uniform, screaming his head off.

He put on a burst of speed, lowered his head, and drove his helmet directly into Curtis Danko's stomach!

Everyone gasped as Curtis fell to the floor. Then Coach Kankel stomped on Curtis's skeleton with his metal cleats.

Curtis's bones crunched under Coach Kankel's feet. He was smashing Curtis to bits!

The room fell silent. Coach Kankel continued to crunch Curtis Danko's bones beneath his feet.

"Ha!" Coach Kankel shouted, flashing his fingers in a "V" for victory. "I got him! I got him! Ding dong, the zombie's dead! And I killed him! I win! I win! I saved the town!"

He danced in front of the crowd, crowing, "Who you gonna call? Bob Churney? I don't think so! Who you gonna call? James Walker? Not! Who you gonna call? Coach Kankel!"

I stared at the coach, then noticed something behind him. Curtis Danko's bones! They were moving together, reforming into the skeleton of Curtis Danko—all by themselves!

"Hahahahaha! Look at me!" Coach Kankel crowed. "I'm king of the world!!!"

Curtis Danko rose from the floor. He tapped Coach Kankel on the shoulder.

Coach Kankel turned, and let out a yelp and cowered behind his wife.

"Nice going, Coach," Sheriff Frady said.

Curtis's broken body clicked and creaked as he made his way back to the pedestal. He stood before the crowd, staring at all of us. His glowing green eyes blazed with light.

Dayna quietly touched my hand. "Danny," she said.

"Yeah?" I answered.

"When he pulls off that shroud—" She paused, searching for words. "If we turn into stone or burst into flames or something, I just wanted you to know—I really liked you."

My heart leaped a little.

"I really liked you, too." I smiled at her.

Curtis Danko's eyes flashed. The whole crowd watched him, waiting to see what he would do.

His bony hand rose in the air. He pointed to the top of the pedestal, where the famous statue now sat, covered in its shroud.

I gripped Dayna's hand.

Curtis gave a signal to one of the zombies. The zombie ripped the shroud from the statue.

I squeezed my eyes shut. I couldn't help it.

I heard the others let out a gasp.

I opened my eyes.

I glanced at the crowd, to see if anyone had burst into flames. But everyone was fine. They stared wide-eyed at the statue.

Then Mrs. Kankel started beating Coach Kankel with her purse. "You stupid, rotten, no-good, jealous weasel!" she shrieked.

Finally I let my eyes drift up toward the statue.

"Oh . . . wow . . ." I breathed. I couldn't believe it. *That* was the statue?

"Isn't that—?" Dayna gasped.

"Yeah," I said, beginning to smile. "It's—"

I couldn't bring myself to say it out loud—I was too amazed.

On top of the pedestal stood Curtis Danko's sculpture—a life-sized statue of a man holding a carved pumpkin under his arm. And the man was—Uncle Fred.

I glanced at Coach Kankel. His face went white.

The whole town turned silent. No one knew what to say. Then a tiny sound came from the statue. *Scritch scritch scritch.* Something was moving inside the pumpkin.

"Aha!" Coach Kankel shouted. "I warned you! But you didn't listen. Here it comes! The evil rises! The end is near!"

The scratchy sound grew louder. A woman screamed. Then the top of the pumpkin flew off! The woman screamed again . . . and a squirrel popped his head up through the hole.

The squirrel chattered and gazed curiously at the crowd. Everyone burst out laughing.

"Do you mean to tell me that all these years we had no Halloween because of this?" Mrs. Kankel demanded. She raised her purse. Coach Kankel shielded his head.

"I don't understand. . . ." Uncle Fred murmured.

"You're a hero, Mr. Walker!" someone shouted.

I realized the voice was Curtis Danko's.

Uncle Fred looked at Curtis. "How could I be a hero—to you?" he asked.

Curtis slowly walked up to Uncle Fred. From underneath his scorched and tattered shirt he pulled an old photo. He held it up for Uncle Fred to see.

I strained to get a glimpse of the picture over Uncle Fred's shoulder. It showed Uncle Fred in his younger days. It looked as if he were a judge at an art fair, standing in front of a wall of paintings. He was handing a blue ribbon to a small, pale boy with wild dark hair. Hovering in the background were some mean-looking boys, frowning. One of the boys looked just like Ryan Kankel—and I knew it must have been his father, Coach Kankel.

Uncle Fred touched the photo lightly. Then he said, "But—I built the kiln. It's my fault you—"

Curtis Danko shook his head. He turned to stare at Coach Kankel. Shaking, Coach Kankel pointed at Sheriff Frady.

"It was an accident! I swear!" Coach Kankel cried.

"You were there?" Dad asked.

"It was just a prank," Coach Kankel insisted.

As he told us his story, I closed my eyes and tried to picture it. Curtis, still alive, was working late at night in the art room at school. Fireflies glowed around him. Suddenly—*thump!* He heard a noise at the window. He turned and saw the top of a ladder resting on the windowsill. Someone was coming!

Curtis picked up his sculpture and slipped into the kiln to hide. He left the door open just a crack, so he could peek through and see who was coming.

Coach Kankel, just a kid then, stuck his face in the crack in the door and yelled, "Boo!" He was trying to scare Curtis. Some other boys—including Sheriff Frady—were with him, egging him on.

Wham! Coach Kankel slammed the kiln door shut. The other boys helped him slide shut the metal bar that locked it. They all started yelling, calling Curtis nasty names.

Then Coach Kankel saw a shadow outside the classroom door. He heard the clatter of keys unlocking it. Startled, everyone hurried to the window and scrambled out.

Coach Kankel grabbed Sheriff Frady by the arm and dragged him out of the art room—just as the janitor opened the door and turned on the lights.

The janitor didn't see the boys escape. He didn't notice much, because he was wearing headphones and listening to loud music while he worked.

The janitor! I thought. Without realizing it, the janitor must have bumped the On button to the kiln!

The burners in the big furnace next to the kiln room ignited. Curtis Danko was locked in the kiln. He couldn't get out—and no one could hear him scream.

"We didn't know the kiln would get turned on!" Coach Kankel finished. "It was an accident!"

Everyone in town was glaring at Coach Kankel. Mrs. Churney shook her finger at him. "But you said you saw the statue when you went into the kiln the next day! You said it was pure evil! You told everyone it was too horrifying to look at!"

Coach Kankel seemed to shrink. "How could I let anyone see that I was wrong all along about Curtis Danko? I had to make him seem bad."

"So *you* wrote the note in the ashes," Dad said. "You wrote the curse! And you came out of the kiln pretending your eyes were burning—and convinced everyone that Curtis was pure evil? Why? *Why?*"

"Because his statue was going to win the contest!" Coach Kankel cried. "And then the image of *your* dad was going to sit in the town square! Not *my* statue of *my* dad!"

A wide, tall, strong-looking zombie with a flat-top hairdo stepped up next to Coach Kankel. "Michael Edward Kankel!" he boomed.

"D-d-d-daddy?" Coach Kankel stammered.

"Don't you d-d-d-daddy me!" Pops Kankel threatened. He towered over Coach Kankel, hands on his hips, scowling.

"But, Dad!" Coach Kankel protested. "You deserve to be the big hero—not Walker!"

"You are in a mess of trouble, boy," Pops Kankel snarled. He grabbed Coach Kankel by the arm and dragged him away. I caught sight of Ryan, who stared after his father with his mouth hanging open.

Everyone at Curtis Danko's house, living and dead, tilted his head up and admired the statue of Uncle Fred. I felt so proud of him. I knew what a good man he was. And I was happy to know that Curtis Danko—and now the whole town—admired him, too.

Curtis gestured toward Uncle Fred, who was standing in the crowd, and began to applaud for him. The other zombies rattled their bony hands together. Then the living clapped for him, too. Uncle Fred bowed slightly and said, "Thank you," to Curtis.

Curtis nodded. Then he turned and walked away through the crowd, heading out of the square. The people of Walker Falls watched him pass with a new respect. I kept watching him until he disappeared in the shadows of the street that led to the cemetery.

The crowd began to break up. Dayna hurried over to the couch, where her mother still sat unconscious. I spotted an old zombie woman standing among the others, staring at Dad. She looked familiar to me, but I wasn't sure. I pointed her out to Dad. He blinked and stared at her, stunned.

"Mom?" he said.

I gasped. It was Grandma Walker!

Uncle Fred spun around to look at her. "Doris?"

The old lady zombie approached us. "Hello, boys. I must look a sight, huh?"

"No!" Uncle Fred protested. "You look good! I mean, you know . . . all things considered."

"You look"—Grandma paused—"like you need some rest."

"How are you feeling, Uncle Fred?" I asked him. I thought he was looking tired, too.

"I'm okay, Danny," he said. "I'm really okay." He turned to Dad and added, "I never felt better. You want to know why?"

Dad nodded.

"Because I finally, really know . . . that I'm loved."

Dad grimaced. "There are 327 pictures up in your old office that should have proved that to you long ago. Pictures of you and generations of kids in this town, just like the one that Curtis Danko gave you—"

"Not by the kids of Walker Falls, James," Uncle Fred said. "By you."

Dad swallowed. I could tell he was getting choked up.

"I was mad at you," Dad said. "For a long time. I just wished you'd spent more time . . ." He blinked back a few tears. ". . . with *me*."

"You were so smart," Uncle Fred explained. "So capable. I didn't think you needed me all that much. . . ." He stared at the photo Curtis Danko had given him. "Not the way other kids, with less, did. I guess I was just trying to be a hero.

"It's too bad we never had this talk before I kicked the bucket," Uncle Fred went on. "That would have been nice."

"It's still nice," Dad said.

A firefly blinked on a nearby branch. Uncle Fred watched it as its glow began to fade.

"After tonight you probably won't see me again," he told us.

My throat felt thick. Tears welled up in my eyes. Dad was blinking and wiping his eyes.

"But I'll see you," Uncle Fred promised. "And I'll be very, very proud. Now, if you'll excuse me, I have one last thing I'd like to do in the time I have left."

"What's that?" Dad asked.

"I'd like to take your mother dancing with the fireflies," Uncle Fred said.

He nodded outside. We all walked toward the old band shell.

A greenish light glowed as rickety zombie couples waltzed. They whirled around and around in a spinning cloud of fireflies.

Dayna and Taylor appeared beside us. Taylor looked as if she'd just woken up from a nap. She smiled at us and touched Dad's hand. Dad's whole face lit up.

"Would you—I mean—" He fumbled for the right words. "Could you ever see yourself . . ."

"Dancing again?" Taylor finished. "Maybe." She leaned against him as we all watched the zombies do their ghostly waltz.

I glanced at Dayna. Was she thinking what I was thinking?

"My mom and your dad—?" she whispered. We giggled. It seemed weird, but in a good way.

A pink light glowed on the horizon—dawn. As the light grew stronger, the zombie couples broke apart. They began to disintegrate into wisps of dust. A light breeze started to blow, carrying the dust up and away.

Uncle Fred and Grandma Walker spun past me in a final dance. Uncle Fred tossed something to me.

I caught it. It was his Red Baron Hot Wheels car.

The rising sun burned brighter than the glow of the fireflies. The bugs dissolved into strands of light that drifted down into the earth. The zombie dancers slowly disappeared. No one was left in town but the living people of Walker Falls. We all stood silently in the square, watching the sunrise.

Beep beeeeep! A blaring car horn made me jump. Dad's BMW screeched into the square and skidded to a stop. Mrs. Vanderspool gripped the wheel, her knuckles white.

"You wouldn't believe what we saw on our way from the airport," she gasped. "Zombies!"

The back doors flew open and out of the car stumbled three German businessmen. They looked exhausted. It had taken them hours to get back from the airport.

One of the Germans broke into a wide grin. "Trick or treat!" he shouted. "Walker Falls has the best Halloween costumes! Those zombies looked so real!"

Dad just nodded.

"Now, about your chocolate factory, Herr Walker," the businessman said. He whipped a checkbook out of his jacket pocket. "We're doubling our investment!"

"All right!" I shouted.

"On one condition," the businessman warned.

"What's that?" Dad asked.

"We put on an even *bigger* Spooktacular next year!" he cried.

The whole town erupted in cheers.

"Whoopee!" I yelled. Dayna and I jumped up and down. I was glad things were working out for Dad. I was beginning to like Walker Falls after all.

"We have a lot of planning to do," the businessman said. "What time shall we start work?"

"Seven A.M.," Dad said. "Bright and early—"

My heart sank and I looked away. I didn't want Dad to see how disappointed I was. He was going to be busy all the time now—and I didn't have Uncle Fred to keep me company anymore.

"—two weeks from now," Dad finished, grinning at me. I gasped and looked up at him to see if he meant it.

"Danny and I have got a shuttle launch to catch," Dad said. "After all, those space-food sticks won't last forever!"

Collect them all— if you dare!